EVENTIDE

Other books by R. A. Steffan

The Last Vampire: Books 1-3
The Last Vampire: Books 4-6

Vampire Bound: Book One
Vampire Bound: Book Two
Vampire Bound: Book Three
Vampire Bound: Book Four

Forsaken Fae: Book One
Forsaken Fae: Book Two
Forsaken Fae: Book Three

The Sixth Demon: Book One
The Sixth Demon: Book Two
The Sixth Demon: Book Three
The Sixth Demon: Book Four

Circle of Blood: Books 1-3
Circle of Blood: Books 4-6

The Complete Horse Mistress Collection
The Complete Lion Mistress Collection
The Complete Dragon Mistress Collection
The Complete Master of Hounds Collection

Antidote: Love and War, Book 1
Antigen: Love and War, Book 2
Antibody: Love and War, Book 3
Anthelion: Love and War, Book 4
Antagonist: Love and War, Book 5

Liminal: The Morpheus Trilogy, Book One

EVENTIDE

R. A. STEFFAN

Eventide: The Morpheus Trilogy, Book Three

ISBN: 978-1-955073-87-5 (paperback)

For more information, contact the author at
http://www.rasteffan.com/contact/

Cover by Ember

First Edition: February 2025

TABLE OF CONTENTS

ONE

HUGH DE FERRERS HAD lived many lives. He'd visited far-flung lands—both earthly and ethereal—and tried his hand at a myriad of skills over the centuries. Somehow, none of it had adequately prepared him for the prospect of becoming a frontline combatant in a war between gods.

Returning to his secluded little cottage in the waking world after the Grim Reaper's revelation about Morpheus' lost sister, the Goddess of Hope, had seemed the natural thing to do. Perhaps it had been foolish, though, since the cottage was a wreck, and Hugh's physical body wasn't in much better shape.

As an immortal, he'd volunteered to die so he could take an important message to Morpheus' uncle in Tartarus, for all the good that had done. In the end, Morpheus had been forced to go and visit Death himself, while Hugh and Iridaceae—Morpheus' shape-shifting owl familiar—had been left behind on Earth to deal with the ugly aftermath.

Remaining with Morpheus in the Night Lands, where the gods resided, would have been far more comfortable than coming back here. In the real world, Hugh's head still hurt from the bottle of vodka he'd swilled to knock himself out, while his chest still hurt from allowing Iridaceae to suffocate him to death with a pillow once he was unconscious.

But after his brief, tempestuous stint as a mortal, Morpheus seemed, oddly, to find some comfort in the rhythms of the Sublunary. Things like the making of tea and the familiarity of a battered kitchen table… at least, once Hugh had swept all the bits of fallen plaster from the floor, counters, and table into a dustpan.

For his part, Hugh had to force himself not to look at the splintered door of the corner pantry, where Morpheus had trapped Iridaceae long enough that he could abscond with Hugh's best kitchen knife and off himself in the woods nearby. He set a mug of tea down in front of his thankfully very-much-living lover and tugged a chair around, so his back was to the broken pantry door.

"I will have to return to my realm," Morpheus said, frowning down at the steaming mug.

He sounded exhausted. As exhausted as Hugh himself felt, despite the hours of sleep he'd had while his soul gallivanted around the Night Lands with his lover.

"Do you want me to come with you?" Hugh asked, still feeling out this tenuous new reality where Morpheus treated him like a true partner instead of a subject.

The God of Dreams was silent for a moment, twisting the warm mug back and forth between his palms.

"It is not necessary," he said at last. "You may join me there whenever you sleep next, if that is amenable."

Hugh sighed. "You don't have to walk on eggshells around me, Morpheus. This thing between us is... new, I know. And I still have no idea how it's going to work, day by day. But I've got things to do here in the cottage—not to mention, I could use a bit of time to think."

He didn't add that he also needed to find out what had happened to the nearby village after some psychotic arsehole had set off a bomb in the old church. Morpheus felt enough guilt over allowing things in the Sublunary to deteriorate under his brother Phobetor's influence, without also reminding him about this latest horror.

His companion nodded slowly. "Very well. I have ensured that your dreams will be lucid unless you wish them not to be. If I am not with you immediately once you fall asleep, come to the palace."

"Palace, got it," Hugh said gamely, hoping the actual logistics of moving around in his dreams would make more sense once he was back in Morpheus' realm.

His lover's crystal-blue gaze settled on him; the noble brow furrowed delicately in worry. "I suppose I do not need to exhort you to take care in the waking world. The danger here grows every day that my brother is allowed to continue unchecked."

"I'm still immortal, *leof*," Hugh reminded him tiredly. "But don't worry. The only thing on my agenda today is cleaning up cracked ceiling plaster and doing some research. Go home. Get your oneiri back in line, if Iridaceae hasn't done it for you already."

"Indeed." Morpheus lifted the mug of tea to his lips and took a long sip, his graceful throat working as he swallowed. Then, to Hugh's surprise, he rose and leaned down, resting his forehead against Hugh's for several seconds. "I am cognizant of the pain I have caused you," he said into their shared air. "I wish never to do that again. However, I am also not so naïve as to believe my efforts going forward will be without their failures."

Hugh had to pick through that rather convoluted declaration for a moment to make certain he'd understood the gist.

"Hey." He lifted a hand to cradle the back of his lover's neck, threading his fingers through the fine hair. "I know you're hurting, too. How about we both just do the best we can for now. We'll iron out the details once the rest of this mess is sorted."

Morpheus straightened with a nearly inaudible huff, and Hugh let him go. "'Once the rest of this mess is sorted,'" he echoed wryly. "As always, I admire your faith, my hunter."

"Hope's what got us into this situation, right?" Hugh said, keeping his tone light. "Maybe hope's what will get us back out, as well."

"There is a pleasing symmetry to the idea," Morpheus agreed. "Goodbye Hugh—until we meet in dreams."

And with that, he stepped into the veil separating the realms, disappearing from view.

◆

One thing about cleaning up the debris in the cottage, it was a pleasantly mindless task. He'd tackled the news reports first, since the uncertainty would only continue to nag at him if he put it off. There was precious little clarity when it came to the death toll in the village. The reporting only said that deaths were confirmed to be in the dozens, with the toll expected to rise over the coming days.

Some of the fires were still burning, as of the most recent updates. Hugh had to forcefully remind himself that from an objective standpoint, very little time had passed since the explosion. Add to that the sorry state of emergency services in a world where emergencies were becoming the norm, and it was no real surprise that answers and factual information were thin on the ground.

The urge to drive down and see if he could help somehow was nearly overwhelming. The idea of a village on fire tugged at the medieval peasant in him, whispering that he should be standing in a bucket line somewhere rather than sweeping and vacuuming up bits of fallen ceiling from his floors.

It murmured that he could be out there making a difference, even if that difference was small. *Save one person*, it said. *Bind one bandage. Put out one fire.*

Ignoring that little voice went against eight hundred years of instinct, because he'd never been the strategist in any of the wars he'd fought in. He'd always been the foot soldier. He was the cog, while others turned the wheel.

The idea that he was currently the only human on Earth with insight into the root cause of the madness was sobering in the extreme. His job now was not to scurry around in the chaos, trying to put small things right after the fact. It was to fix the underlying issue, cutting the madness off at its source.

He couldn't imagine anyone worse suited to the task. Too bad that trying to explain the situation to people who might be *better* suited—scientists, philosophers, the news media—would probably get him sectioned for suspected mental health issues.

"They might not even be wrong about me," he muttered, dumping another heaping dustpan full of plaster bits into the rubbish bin.

The entire thing sounded utterly mad. The Goddess of Hope had reneged on her duties and run away to live with a human lover, long before even *Hugh* had been born. She'd hidden her divinity in a clay jar so she could become mortal, just as Morpheus had foolishly done with an opal pendant not so very long ago.

And then, someone had come along and broken the jar, scattering its contents into the ether… leaving the mortal realm without Hope's avatar. Hugh idly swept up another dustpan full of debris, wondering if the clay jar had been broken purposely or accidentally. Had the goddess Elpis done it herself, to sever ties with the Night Lands for good? Or had someone done it against her will?

Whoever it was that destroyed the jar, had they understood what would happen with hope gone from the world?

He picked up the dustpan and headed back to the bin. "Hope escaping from a jar? It's like bloody Pandora's box in reverse," he grumbled.

Abruptly, his brain registered what he'd just said, galloping ahead down the tenuous chain of logic.

The Greek gods were real. They were fucking *real*. He'd bedded one of them, for god's —

For... *someone's* sake.

The dustpan slipped from his slack grip and clattered to the floor, plaster dust billowing out of it to spatter his trouser legs in white powder.

"Holy shit. Pandora's box was *real*," he whispered, standing frozen in place for a moment before tearing himself free and lurching toward the bathroom.

He needed the strongest sleeping pills in the house, and he needed them *now*.

TWO

IT WAS STILL EARLY in the region of the Sublunary Hugh called home, and Morpheus had not expected the human's return to the land of dreams for some time yet. He glanced up in surprise from the mirror he'd been examining, as the sound of unexpected bootsteps echoed against flagstone. On his shoulder, Iridaceae twisted her head around and gave a happy hoot of greeting.

"Wow," Hugh said, looking around the throne room with wide eyes. "Okay… I don't think I truly understood the scope of this place before. Are there… an *infinite* number of mirrors in here?"

Morpheus frowned, glancing at the familiar walls of his throne room. "Hardly infinite. These are the windows into the minds of my dreamers, and there are not an infinite number of creatures that dream."

Hugh turned in a slow circle. "Huh. I think we might have stumbled over a god-human divide, in that case. As far as my brain is concerned, these walls go on forever in every direction."

"Interesting," Morpheus said, mildly intrigued. "Though I can assure you they do not."

"So, you can really keep track of all this stuff at once?" Hugh asked. "Because infinite or no, that's impressive, to put it mildly."

Morpheus gave a small shrug, sending Iridaceae's wings fluttering as she rebalanced herself. "It is my function. Without dreams, I would not exist."

"And without you around, dreams gradually fall apart," Hugh said thoughtfully. "Which brings me to what I need to talk to you about, I suppose." He gave the walls a last, wary look before focusing his attention firmly on Morpheus. "I might have some new insight about what happened to your sister."

Iridaceae flapped down to the floor, transforming as she landed. "You do?" she said, before Morpheus could reply. "That was fast!"

"What sort of insight?" Morpheus asked.

"The mythological kind," Hugh said, warming to his topic. "I assume you're familiar with the story of Pandora's box?"

Morpheus scanned his memory of human dreams. "A rather misogynistic morality tale from the first millennium B.C., regarding the dangers of indulging idle curiosity?"

"And the dangers of trusting women, yes," Hugh replied. "Specifically, though—it's a misogynistic morality tale from the first millennium B.C. wherein the main character opens a mysterious jar left in her care, inadvertently releasing every evil into the world. After which, she realizes what she's done and quickly closes it, leaving only hope behind in the container. Am I crazy, or is that too much of a coincidence to be unrelated to your sister's fate?"

Morpheus opened his mouth to speak, paused for a moment, and closed it again.

Iridaceae tilted her head, birdlike. "But... isn't that the opposite of what happened to Elpis? Her godhood was the only thing stored in the jar. *That's* what was scattered into the world. Not a bunch of evil things."

Mind racing with new possibilities, Morpheus slowly shook his head back and forth. "No. That may well be the literal interpretation of what occurred, if the Titans in the pit are to be believed. However, an argument might be made that by destroying my sister's godhood, whoever broke the jar *did* release new strife into the world."

"That's what I was thinking," Hugh agreed. "Like you said, it's a morality tale. Pandora's box was never meant to be literal… although I'm starting to wonder if it's a lot more literal than I ever gave it credit for being."

Iridaceae crossed her arms and huffed. "All right. But if Pandora's box was Elpis' jar, does that help us at all? It's still broken. Or, y'know, *open*. If it was actually a box with a lid."

"The word 'box' was a mistranslation," Hugh said. "I did a bit of research while I was waiting for the sleeping pills to kick in. It was called a *pithos* in the original texts from Hesiod. A bloke in the sixteenth century changed it to *pyxis* — a box. A *pithos* is a clay storage jar. I should know — I dug up enough of the damned things when I was on an archaeology kick in the early nineteen hundreds."

More possibilities and probabilities flickered through Morpheus' awareness, too fast to catalogue. "It is certainly suggestive," he allowed.

Hugh nodded. "Isn't it just? Now, what I'm wondering is this. The myth specifically says that hope was left behind in the box. Or rather, in the *pithos*. But we know that, in reality, Elpis' godhood was scattered and lost. Is there any possibility that the jar itself—whatever's left of it, anyway—still holds traces of her powers somehow? Meaning, could the actual physical item be useful to us in some way?"

"What, you think some of her godhood soaked into the jar like wine stains?" Iridaceae sounded understandably skeptical.

"I suppose it is possible," Morpheus mused. "For one thing, the *pithos* could not have been a normal jar made of fired clay, manufactured by a human. Such an object would not possess even a fraction of the capacity necessary to store a god's power."

"Okay, I'm confused," Hugh said. "Your opal was far smaller than a jar, and you fit your godhood into it, didn't you?"

Morpheus smiled a thin smile, not pleased to revisit the details of his own foolishness and lack of foresight—but aware that it was necessary. "You conflate physical size with capacity. Opal is an amorphous mineraloid. It is less rigid than faceted gems. Its structure extends into dimensions humans cannot access or perceive, allowing for an extensive amount of storage in the spaces between the atoms and subatomic particles."

Hugh frowned, his expression growing thoughtful. "So, Elpis or someone else would have needed to make this jar specially so that it could hold her power?"

"One assumes so." Morpheus turned and started pacing.

Hugh was still thinking aloud. "That's good, though, isn't it? It would mean we might have some way to distinguish the remains of *this* jar from every other collection of pottery shards in existence, right? Because—I won't lie—the odds of finding one broken jar sound like they would barely be one step up from impossibility. Bad enough if it's warehoused in some random museum's collection, but..."

"What if it's still buried in the dirt somewhere?" Iridaceae finished.

"Or what if it's been crushed to dust beneath the ravages of time?" Hugh added sourly.

Morpheus paused in his restless pacing, coming to a decision. "The parallels between my sister's loss and the details of this myth are striking. However, I do not believe it will be productive to dive into an immediate search in the Sublunary. Not in the absence of more detailed information regarding the truth behind the story."

Hugh hesitated. "Agreed," he said. "In principle, at least. But... I'm afraid I don't see how you're going to track down any new information about something that happened well before the birth of Christ. Do you plan to talk to scholars, or archaeologists, or—"

Morpheus scoffed. "Nothing so pedestrian. As you correctly point out, all the humans involved are long dead."

"Well, yes..." Hugh broke off and winced. "Oh. They're *dead*. You don't mean..."

"If this Pandora ever existed as a real individual," Morpheus continued, "she will be found in only one place, assuming her soul has not moved on to oblivion."

Hugh sighed. "So, Tartarus again?"

"Indeed," Morpheus confirmed, bracing himself to once more confront his uncle, the God of Death.

THREE

HUGH HAD A SNEAKING suspicion that he and Morpheus had worn out their welcome with Thanatus, the God of Death, some time ago. This suspicion was further reinforced when they arrived to find the deity in question rebuilding a supporting wall of his castle. Specifically, the supporting wall that Morpheus had transformed into a flock of birds in a fit of rage during their last visit.

The dark figure looked up, scowling. "You try my patience, Morpheus."

"As you try *mine*, Uncle," Morpheus retorted.

"Are you familiar with the human myth of Pandora's Box?" Hugh asked, in an attempt to fast-forward past the familial squabbling.

Thanatus looked at him blankly. "No."

"Oh," Hugh said. "Well, that certainly complicates matters."

"We require an interview with the soul of the woman in question." Morpheus told him.

"Assuming she actually exists," Hugh muttered.

"Why?" Thanatus asked in a wary tone. "What is the content of this myth?"

"That would be an interesting question to ask the Titans in the pit," Morpheus said. "Perhaps you will do so, as they would also be the most likely to know about the fate of the titular character's soul."

Thanatus settled a heavy gaze on him. "Is this about your sister?"

"Of course it's about his bloody sister!" Hugh snapped, unable to stop himself. "Unlike other members of this family, *he* gives a damn that the Sublunary is in chaos!"

Thanatus' attention never wavered from his nephew. Given that Hugh was allergic to dying, that probably should've been a relief. Instead, it just pissed him off more.

"I've already told you, there's nothing to be done about the situation," said the God of Death.

"And yet," Morpheus replied, "it has taken less than a day in the mortal realm for Hugh to uncover a tangible link to Elpis."

"Balderdash." Thanatus looked momentarily taken aback.

"Pandora's Box. Ask the Titans." Morpheus didn't so much as blink.

Thanatus glared at him. "You impudent little…"

"We'll wait here for your return, shall we?"

This was probably not an appropriate time for Hugh to find his lover's air of casual impudence kind of hot.

The two gods stared each other down, blue eyes locked with obsidian. And then, without a word, Thanatus vanished in a swirl of inky vapor. When he didn't immediately reappear to yell at them some more, Hugh gave into temptation and turned, catching Morpheus around the nape of the neck and pressing their lips together in a brief, filthy kiss.

Morpheus made a startled noise, a look of confusion marring his brow when Hugh pulled back.

"Apparently I have a thing for sexy gods laying down the law," Hugh told him by way of explanation. "So, do we think he's gone to talk to the monsters in the pit? Or gone to gather an army of terrifying zombies to eat our brains as punishment for bothering him again?"

"Almost certainly the former," Morpheus said, regaining control of his expression. "I implied, indirectly at least, that the Titans have been withholding information from him regarding Elpis' destruction. He will not have liked that possibility."

"Hmm," Hugh said. "Hope you're right." He eyed the half-repaired castle wall. "I suppose it'd be juvenile to turn that wall into, I dunno, lizards or toads or something while he's gone."

"Yes," Morpheus said with finality. "It would be."

Hugh made a theatrical noise of disappointment. They waited. The shadowy forms of curious shades slunk around the edges of the room, watching them. Hugh couldn't help a small shudder as one of the creatures darted in for a closer look.

"*Shoo*," Morpheus told it.

When Thanatus returned, he drew a dark wisp of melancholy from his robes and tossed it to the ground. The God of Death was visibly seething, his white teeth clenched together.

"The soul who spawned the legend is gone," he spat.

"She chose oblivion?" Morpheus asked. "Then... who was this remnant when he lived?"

Hugh couldn't have said why his mind interpreted the dark smear on the floor as *cowering*, but at the words, it cringed further in on itself.

"This was the woman's husband," Thanatus bit out. "His soul has been languishing in the pit for millennia."

Morpheus looked up at him sharply. "Why was his essence not crushed out of existence long ago?"

Thanatus waved a hand in disgust. "Apparently he is a mixed-breed descendant of Iapetus."

"Who's Iapetus when he's at home?" Hugh asked.

"Another one of the Titans," Morpheus said, glancing over at him. "Though not one of the ones trapped in the pit." He turned his full attention on the wispy remnant. "I begin to see why the Cyclopes and the Hundred-Handers took such an interest in this tale."

"Family drama?" Hugh offered, struggling to see how any of this tied together in a useful way.

"Perhaps," Morpheus agreed. He reached down, settling his hand over the shifting edges of the tortured soul. A pale glow surrounded the remnant, which shifted and grew in stature until the ghostly outline of an elderly man in primitive clothing stood before them. "Now, tell me, husband of Pandora—what is your name?"

"My name is Epimetheus," the spirit rasped. "But my wife's name was Anesidora, not Pandora."

"Another variation in the legend," Hugh said. "If Wikipedia is to be believed, anyway."

"Very well, Epimetheus." Morpheus eyed the ghost critically. "You have suffered for a long time in the pit. Tell us what has weighed on you so heavily for all these centuries."

Epimetheus gazed at them with the air of someone who had been waiting an eternity to properly air his grievances.

"My wife," the ghost blurted. "She was unfaithful to me."

Hugh and Morpheus shared a look. Hugh very pointedly didn't roll his eyes.

"Go on," Morpheus said.

The spirit wrung its spectral hands together. "I came home early from a journey and found Anesidora lying with another woman in our marriage bed. I killed them both in a rage before they could escape."

"Lovely," Hugh muttered, with a slow, sinking feeling. "Don't suppose you got the other woman's name first?"

The ghost looked at Hugh like he was an idiot. "No. Why would I?"

"Continue, please," Morpheus said. "What happened next?"

Epimetheus wrapped nonexistent arms around his nonexistent body, huddling in on himself. "My anger was not assuaged by their deaths. I was compelled to destroy any object that my wife cared for. I smashed statues and defaced mosaics. I broke furniture and snapped hair ornaments. And..." He trailed off.

"Yes?" Morpheus prompted.

"There was a painted clay jar," Epimetheus continued in a rush. "My wife kept it on a shelf above our bed—a plain thing, but she always ensured it was dusted and displayed in pride of place. I shattered it. But the instant the seal broke—"

He cut himself off with a soft choking noise.

"You knew you had done something horrible," Morpheus finished for him.

Epimetheus nodded rapidly, his head bobbing forward and back. "I felt everything around me change, and I knew it was all my fault. I hid the shards of the jar in a cave and fled my comfortable life to live alone in the forest until Death came for me."

"I see," Morpheus said, doing a surprisingly good job of keeping his crackling anger leashed. "Tell me—this cave where you hid the remains of the broken jar. Could you find it again?"

Thanatus, who had been watching the exchange from the sidelines, bristled. "Nephew..." he said warningly.

But Morpheus held up a quelling hand, his whole focus on the wavering outline of the spirit.

Epimetheus swallowed, his Adam's apple bobbing. "I... believe so, yes."

"Very well, then," Morpheus told him. "We will leave immediately."

FOUR

THANATUS ROSE TO his full height. *"You will do no such thing."*

Morpheus was aware of the impropriety of his actions—barging into the realm of another, more powerful god and making demands of him. The God of Death had dominion over the souls under his care in a way that Morpheus and his brothers did not. A mortal creature could experience fear or fantasy while they were dreaming. They could awaken, leaving his realm entirely.

Once a living being died, however, their existence belonged to Tartarus and its ruler—until and unless they faded into oblivion for eternity. For Morpheus to stroll in and announce that he was leaving with the soul of a denizen of the Pit was the height of hubris. And yet…

He reached out and gathered up the thin essence of Epimetheus, binding the remnant to him. Thanatus stared at him in open-mouthed shock. Given the danger Morpheus was courting by openly defying his uncle in such a way, he probably shouldn't have found the expression so satisfying.

Bracing himself to shove Hugh back to wakefulness and out of the Night Lands should his bluff be called, Morpheus straightened, squaring his shoulders.

"We are leaving, Uncle. Unless you wish to strike me down where I stand, you have no further say in the matter. Phobetor must be stopped. The Sublunary must be saved. As you will take no direct action toward those ends, it falls to me and mine to do so." With that, he turned his back on Thanatus, aware that there was a small but non-zero possibility it would be the last action he ever took. "Come, Hugh. We are leaving."

"Where—" Hugh began, but Morpheus nudged him toward his sleeping body in the mortal realm. His dream-self faded away, and Morpheus followed him through the veil with Epimetheus' stolen soul in tow.

He reappeared in Hugh's familiar bedroom, where the human groaned and rolled over on his bed. He blinked fully awake, his eyes bloodshot and his expression groggy.

"*Argh.* Bloody sleeping pills," he slurred. Then he sat up clumsily, catching himself against the headboard. "Hang on. Did you just abduct a dead Greek bloke from the underworld?"

"I suppose you could characterize it that way," Morpheus said.

Hugh scowled. "Isn't that, y'know, frowned on? I *have* read other myths besides Pandora's, Morpheus."

"I believe we are past the point of observing the social niceties. Even those of the Night Lands."

Hugh stared at him for a long moment. Then he shrugged and rubbed at one eye with the heel of his hand as though his head pained him. "Okay. Fair."

"We must discuss our next move," Morpheus told him, still unused to the necessity of seeking another person's approval before acting.

Hugh let his hand fall back to the bed. "Yeah. About that. If I've got this straight, Mr. Anger

Management here—" He gestured at Morpheus' robes, indicating the soul held within. " —is going to lead you to some random cave located in, one assumes, Greece. Meanwhile, I'm still a flesh puppet who has to deal with things like passports, and airline booking, and taxis... all while the world is falling down around our ears."

"Yes," Morpheus replied cautiously.

"Whereas you can simply step through the veil from one place to another," Hugh continued. "Which is a really useful trick, by the way. My point being, you should just go. Find the cave, retrieve the MacGuffin, and bring it back here without all the hassle of dealing with customs and border agents."

Morpheus blinked at him, taken aback. "You are certain? You do not wish to accompany me on the journey?"

Hugh rested his elbows loosely on his knees, looking up at him. "Whether I want to come with you is beside the point. Is what you're doing likely to be dangerous?"

"For a god? No," Morpheus said, still skeptical that this conversation could truly be so simple. "Either the cave will still be there, or it will not. Either the shards will be where Epimetheus left them, or they will not."

"And no one else has the faintest idea about their existence, much less their importance," Hugh finished for him. "So, *go*. The fate of the world is more important than my irrational paranoia about letting you out of my sight."

Morpheus watched him intently for a long moment.

"You are a most extraordinary human," he said at length.

"Yup, that's me," Hugh agreed easily. "I also make a really good quiche."

This, too, was accurate. Eating, as a mortal, had been one of many revelations Morpheus had experienced after losing his opal pendant.

"That is true," he said. "Very well. I will return here as quickly as possible."

With no reason to hold back, he leaned a hand on the edge of the bed and captured his human lover's lips with his. Hugh made a startled, appreciative noise before melting into the kiss. One callused palm came up to cup Morpheus' jaw, and for the briefest of moments, he considered postponing his journey for half an hour in favor of covering Hugh's pliant, sleep-drugged body with his own and bringing them both to the sweet, uncomplicated oblivion of sexual release.

Reluctantly, he eased away from the kiss.

"Really need to get you back in this bed once we're not facing down the end of the world," Hugh muttered, as though reading his mind.

"I will hold you to that," Morpheus agreed, and stepped through the veil before he could succumb to temptation.

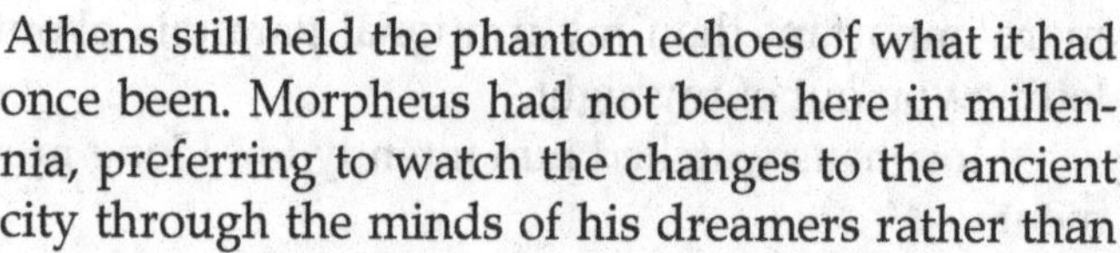

Athens still held the phantom echoes of what it had once been. Morpheus had not been here in millennia, preferring to watch the changes to the ancient city through the minds of his dreamers rather than seeing them in person. It was the middle of the night in Greece; the bones of the Parthenon were illuminated with warm yellow lighting.

The Acropolis was silent except for the eerie whisper of wind among the marble columns — free of tourists at this late hour. Morpheus reached into his robes and extracted the remnant he'd bound. With a thought, he once more leant Epimetheus enough raw dreamstuff to manifest as a translucent, human-shaped spirit.

The ghost looked around, open-mouthed, taking in the ravages of time and the marvels of electric spotlights illuminating the scene.

"We are in Athens," Morpheus told him. "Orient yourself. Where is the cave in which you hid the broken *pithos*?"

Through the link he had forged when he bound the man's spirit, Morpheus saw a route form. West, across the Isthmus of Corinth. South, toward Epidaurus. A fine home set among olive orchards... abandoned in haste in favor of the nearby mountainous wilderness. He allowed the spirit to pull him toward their destination, skirting the edges of the mortal realm like a flat stone skipping across still water.

The mountains where they fetched up remained untamed land, with no sign of modern encroachment. Morpheus dared to hope that the cave, too, remained undisturbed, at least by human hands. The intervening centuries were a mere tick of the clock in geologic time, but that didn't mean an earthquake or rockslide could not have collapsed the entrance... or crushed the cavern completely.

Epimetheus led the way with the surety of one seeing what had been in the past, rather than what existed in the present. Morpheus allowed himself to be led.

They ended up at the base of a rocky slope, covered in scree. "It's here," said the spirit, pointing at the fallen rocks.

Morpheus reached out with all his senses.

"Yes. There is a void behind the rubble," he decided. "Come."

For the first time, the spirit balked. "I do not wish to see the jar again."

"I'm certain your wife and my sister did not wish to see you descending on them with murderous intent, either," Morpheus said. "And yet, here we both are."

"Your… *sister*?" the ghost echoed. "I killed your sister?"

Morpheus stepped sideways through the barrier of stone without answering, dragging Epimetheus with him. The interior of the cavern was, as might be expected, pitch black. Morpheus cast a ball of glowing light to hover above their heads.

"Where did you place the shards?" he demanded, plucking the answer from long-buried memory rather than waiting for the wraith to speak aloud.

The entrance had been destroyed, but the small alcove at the back of the cavern remained. Water seeping through limestone had curtained the natural shelf with shining strands of sparkling minerals, like shiny wax dripping from a spent candle.

Still, the ghost hung back.

Morpheus snapped the slender stalactites with his bare hands, widening the opening. Inside lay six dusty, sharp-edged objects like three-dimensional puzzle pieces. Four were rounded and wider at one end. The final two formed the halves of a narrow neck, flared at the top and irregularly broken at the bottom.

Reaching into the cramped alcove, Morpheus withdrew the largest piece. He wasn't certain what he'd expected. Aside from the thin layer of dust, the shard appeared untouched by the passage of time. However, the echo of power he'd half-hoped to feel embedded in the clay was notably absent.

It appeared to be a simple potsherd, nothing more.

And in that moment, Morpheus could think of no more terrible outcome.

"You understand now?" Epimetheus asked, with the air of someone who knew exactly how disastrous his actions had been. "Do you see? You'll fix this for me, won't you?"

A small part of Morpheus wanted to rage at him. How was he to *fix* the murder of his sister in her lover's bed? But that wasn't what Epimetheus was asking. The man had squandered the world's hope in a fit of jealous anger. Guilt over his actions had trapped him in the Pit for thousands of years, bound there by his own regrets.

"Yes," Morpheus said. "I will try." Because what other answer was there, in the end?

"Thank you," Epimetheus whispered, and faded away into the ether. Within seconds, there was nothing left of the tortured soul.

Morpheus stared at the place where the ghost had been for some time. Then he gathered up the broken pieces of the *pithos* and stepped back through the veil, alone.

FIVE

HUGH STARED DOWN at the pieces of broken pottery on his kitchen table. "On the one hand, it doesn't really look like much, does it?" he said. "But on the other hand, it's almost unbelievable that you pulled these shards out of a partially collapsed cave in this condition, after however many thousand years it's been."

He cautiously reached out to touch the nearest piece, glancing at Morpheus first to make sure he wasn't about to get his head blown off or his hand dissolved by magic or something.

He hadn't been joking when he'd mentioned going through an archaeology phase at the start of the previous century. During that period, he'd dusted off more than his share of clay pottery bits. And as a rule, they did *not* maintain glossy painted decorations after lying wherever they'd fallen for centuries or millennia.

"Yes," Morpheus agreed, standing a step back from the table with his arms crossed and his brow furrowed. "There is no question that it was formed and fired by a deity."

Hugh carefully put down the shard he'd picked up. "So, that's *good*, right? It's almost certainly the *pithos* we were looking for."

"I suppose it must be," Morpheus replied.

Hugh met his eyes. "I'm sensing a decided lack of enthusiasm, here."

Morpheus pivoted and paced across the kitchen with precise movements, coming to a stop in front of the ruined pantry door that Hugh still hadn't had the time or emotional energy to fix.

"There is no trace of deific power within the clay," he said, directing the words at the splintered wood. "I can feel nothing of my sister in the remains of this vessel."

The vessel in question sat silent and innocent on the tabletop, almost mocking Hugh with its lack of easy answers.

"All right," he said slowly. "Could that be because it's broken, though? Maybe we could… fix it, somehow?"

Morpheus turned back to him. "I suppose that is the logical next step."

Hugh thought about masking tape and epoxy; the likely end result an ugly caricature of what the vessel had once been.

"I guess I could try," he said reluctantly. "But I'm not sure that's the right way to go about it, given what this object represents. The myth says that the god Hephaestus was the one who originally made the thing. Of course, it also said he's the one who fashioned Pandora herself out of clay, so I'm not entirely certain that's a reliable source."

Morpheus shook his head. "It is moot. Hephaestus was cast out of the Night Lands. There has been no word of him in a very long time."

Hugh's shoulders sagged. "Oh. Okay. Any other gods around who are good with crafts and don't hate your guts?"

His companion returned to the table, running a fingertip delicately over one of the sharp, broken edges of the *pithos*. "Humans have taken over the reins of their own creativity. They gallop ahead faster than the gods, now that they have the bit between their teeth."

Hugh thought about that for a moment. "So… maybe we should find a human to do it. But what if they made the repairs in the Night Lands?"

Morpheus looked sharply at him. "How do you mean?"

Hugh felt the words out, even as he was saying them. "Like, what if you found a master craftsman through their dreams and tasked them with repairing the thing while they slept? Is that something you could do? Because then, it would be a human doing the work, but it would be physically happening in the realm of the gods, where it was originally made."

"Interesting." The little divot between Morpheus' brows deepened for a moment. "I suppose it would be possible, yes."

"In that case, I have a suggestion," Hugh said, the rightness of the sudden idea taking him by surprise. "Japanese kintsugi. Do you know of it?"

Morpheus got that far away, internally focused look that meant he was communing with the collective unconscious. "The repair of broken ceramics using gold. Or, more accurately, the repair of broken ceramics using several different varieties of specialized lacquer which is then decorated with a final layer of gold dust or powder."

"Yes, that." Hugh prodded at the idea more intently, trying to understand the shape of it even as it manifested in his thoughts. "Look, I don't claim to know the science of how you lot stick your god powers inside an inanimate object. But this object is broken, and you say you can't feel any echoes of your sister in the shards. Kintsugi is all about finding the beauty and utility in imperfection."

"Fascinating." Morpheus appeared taken aback.

Hugh plowed onward. "We could try to fix it and hide the repairs… make the *pithos* look as close as possible to how it did before it was broken. But it would be an illusion. This way, maybe the fact that it was shattered simply becomes part of its history. Not good or bad, just something that happened on its journey to us."

Morpheus pulled out a chair and sat down, gazing at the pieces with blue-eyed intensity. "Your suggestion has merit, my hunter. What is broken can never again be unbroken—but broken things may still have value."

"Lucky for both of us, eh?" Hugh joked weakly.

Morpheus gave a quiet snort. "Indeed."

He steepled his fingers and rested his chin on them, glaring down at the potsherds as though he could force them to reform under the weight of his gaze.

"Next question," Hugh said. "Let's jump ahead and pretend we somehow succeed in getting Elpis' scattered powers back in the jar. Not to be cruel about it, but Elpis is long gone. Since she was mortal at the time, I assume that means there's no get-out-of-death-free card. What do we actually do with those recovered powers once we have them?"

Morpheus let his hands drop to the table, clasping them loosely together. "That part, at least, I can answer. Should we be successful—which is far from a given—I will have to take on my sister's powers and responsibilities in addition to my own."

Hugh paused, startled. He wasn't certain what he'd expected Morpheus to say... but it hadn't been that. "You can do that?"

"I see no reason why not," Morpheus replied. "Becoming the dual embodiment of both hopes and dreams may give me sufficient power to contain Phobetor, even given his current ascendency within the mortal realm."

An unpleasant queasy sensation took up residence in Hugh's stomach, and this time he couldn't credibly blame it on the bottle of vodka.

"We really are talking about a war here, aren't we," he said. "A proper one, where you—and I, if I can figure out how to actually do it—will have to fight Phobetor directly."

"Yes," Morpheus replied simply.

Hugh thought of the times when Phobetor had felled him with nothing more than a look, reducing him to gibbering terror or unconsciousness without effort. His stomach roiled harder.

"I knew that," he muttered, coming to stand next to Morpheus' seated form. "I *did*, but..."

Morpheus tilted his head up to meet Hugh's gaze. "Do not allow my brother to land a blow against you before we even reach the field of battle, Hugh."

And that was the crux, wasn't it? Fear was Phobetor's weapon, and here Hugh was, pointing it at his own foot and pulling the trigger.

He was immortal, and he was standing in his house in the middle of a forest with no one around for miles. Even if the world was going progressively madder around him, here and now, there was nothing to be afraid of.

"Sorry," he said. "You're right. No reason to go borrowing trouble before it arrives at our doorstep."

"Quite so," Morpheus agreed. He returned his attention to the broken pottery. "In fact, at this moment I am more concerned about the logistics of gathering my sister's scattered power, should we find ourselves with a vessel capable of collecting and containing it."

"I think I can help with that part," Hugh said, feeling on firmer ground here. "See if you can get this thing repaired first. And then, we've got a standing invitation to one of the few places where I still feel the warmth of hope when I visit."

SIX

KIMURA TAKAO DREAMED of broken things. Morpheus had devoted hours to sifting through the minds of likely artisans before being drawn to this particular mirror, where a wizened old man hunched over a spotless white table, painstakingly continuing his work even while asleep.

Morpheus inserted himself seamlessly into the dream, conjuring a chair and sitting down opposite the elderly craftsman to watch him work. Mr. Kimura glanced up at him, scowled, and immediately incorporated his presence into the vision.

The piece he was working on appeared to be a very ancient teapot that had cracked just below the spout. But every time he rotated the broken pieces to align them, the edges shifted, failing to match up. The deep wrinkles between Mr. Kimura's snow-white brows grew deeper, and he looked up at Morpheus suspiciously, as though he suspected the God of Dreams of purposely playing a prank on him.

Of course, the physical impossibility of the ever-shifting fragments was nothing more than the natural expression of his mind's frustration over a difficult project in the waking world—but a dreamer would have no way of knowing that unless they slipped into lucidity during REM sleep.

Morpheus watched in silence as the artisan struggled to make sense of the nonsensical whimsy of dreams. Eventually, the old man's face cleared in understanding.

"Ah," he said. "How foolish of me. These fragments are from two different teapots. Of course they resist being joined."

With that, he reached behind himself to a shelf that had appeared out of nowhere, retrieving a second broken spout that fit seamlessly to the teapot on the table. After setting the original spout aside, he continued his work, cleverly joining the pieces with a complex series of adhesive lacquers and, finally, decorating the resulting irregular pattern of lines with powdered silver.

"There. Ready for use once more." He carefully placed the finished piece on the table, dream logic conveniently skipping past the extensive curing time that would have been necessary in the waking world. Sharp brown eyes pinned Morpheus. "What say you, my silent observer?"

Morpheus raised an eyebrow. "A difficult repair. You say the teapot will be usable again?"

Mr. Kimura shrugged. "Of course. What a sad world this would be if a single accident or moment of inattention rendered an object permanently useless."

Morpheus spared a moment's thought for the sheer volume of waste he had seen during his foray as a mortal in the Sublunary. "Indeed."

The dreamer sat back in his chair. "Hmm. I feel as though I am being tested. Why is that?"

Reassured of the artisan's prowess within his own dreams, Morpheus drew out the cloth-wrapped bundle containing the shards of his sister's *pithos*.

"I find myself in need of your services," he said, laying them out on the table.

Mr. Kimura stared down at the broken potsherds. "Oh," he breathed, picking up the largest piece with careful fingers. "*Oh*. This is…"

He trailed off, turning the pottery fragment back and forth.

"In need of repair," Morpheus suggested. "Its destruction was not an accident, but it will be a sad and hopeless world indeed if a moment of destructive anger has rendered *this* object permanently useless."

Mr. Kimura's expression sharpened intently as he placed the shard back amongst its brethren.

"Yes, I can see that," he mused, and Morpheus felt a moment's excitement at the idea that this mortal might have sensed something from the *pithos* that he had not—as unlikely as that seemed.

"I wish you to mend this vessel," Morpheus said. "You may work here for as long as you need. All of the resources within my realm are at your disposal."

Mr. Kimura placed his hands palm down on either side of the pile of shards, the pose contemplative. "This piece is not Japanese. By rights, it should be repaired to museum specifications, given its obvious age."

Again, Morpheus was struck by the idea that this human dreamer was not seeing the *pithos* in the same way he did. "Is its age truly so obvious?"

"Oh, yes," said Mr. Kimura. "One gains a sense for these things, with time. But, again, I am not certain it is appropriate to practice the art of kintsugi on Grecian pottery."

"The repairs a museum conservator might perform would not return the vessel to utility," Morpheus said. "This *pithos* belonged to my sister. It is important that it is once more able to contain what she originally placed inside it."

Bony fingers tapped the table lightly — a thoughtful rhythm. Morpheus could see the appeal of the challenge taking root within the old artisan's subconscious mind.

"I suppose it depends on what it originally held," Mr. Kimura said eventually. "However, if this is a family piece and not a museum piece, then I suppose it is your right to decide what is done with it. I will take the commission, as long as you understand that the vessel you end up with will not be the same as the vessel that belonged to your sister."

Morpheus desperately needed it to be the same vessel it had once been. However, the universe cared little for his needs.

"My sister is long gone," he said heavily. "This is all that remains of her. I may wish her to return as she once was… but time does not work like that. Perhaps her legacy was always intended to incorporate change."

"Change is certainly unavoidable," Mr. Kimura agreed philosophically. "Very well. I will attempt to honor your sister's past while also incorporating your future." He paused. "Perhaps you would care to choose the finish on the repairs. Gold is traditional, but many people prefer something a bit more personalized."

"Yes," Morpheus said. "In fact, I have just the thing."

———————◆———————

Morpheus returned to Hugh's cottage in the Sublunary three nights later, the repaired *pithos* cradled in the crook of his arm.

"You're back!" Hugh exclaimed. "I was starting to worry. I tried to visit your palace the last two nights, but Iridaceae said you weren't there. I wasn't entirely sure if it was real, or if I was just having normal dreams."

"Normal dreams *are* real," Morpheus replied distractedly, placing the clay jar on Hugh's kitchen table.

Baphometh, who had been curled up in one of the chairs, hopped up to investigate.

"*Oh*, no," Hugh said, shooing him away. "Nuh-uh. No cliched *'cats knocking things off tables.'* Not to-day."

They both looked down at the *pithos*, taking in the spidering network of glittering lines that now decorated the clay.

Hugh tilted his head. "That's not gold or silver. What is it?"

"The crushed remains of the opal I used to store my powers," Morpheus said. "It seemed an obvious way to increase the likelihood that the jar might once again perform its original function."

"Smart." Hugh leaned closer. "Beautiful, as well—although I don't suppose looks ultimately matter much in this case. This way, part of the jar already knows you, so to speak. I suppose that will help when it comes time for you to absorb your sister's powers?"

"I have absolutely no idea," Morpheus said. "At present, I am more concerned about the logistics of gathering those scattered powers from the ether."

Being very careful to give the *pithos* a wide berth, Hugh leaned forward and pressed his lips to Morpheus'.

"Yes," he said, after pulling back. "About that. You and I are expected for a visit to Mary Walthorpe's stable yard. We're making good on that offer of a pleasant hack through the countryside, during which we're going to hear all about that esteemed matriarch's hopes and plans for her family's future. We just need to rig up some kind of a pack for you to carry this thing around while we do it." He gestured at the jar. "At least it's small."

It was such an insignificant thing amongst all the fear and destruction in the waking world—one family's hope for the coming years. And yet, even beneath Phobetor's boot heel, that same tender shoot of longing for better things must still exist the world over, in myriad different places and myriad different ways.

Morpheus nodded. "Very well. If nothing else, perhaps we can confirm whether the *pithos* will hold hope gathered from mortals, as it once held Elpis' powers. Until then, you should rest as much as possible. The coming days may be busy ones."

Hugh drew him in for another kiss. "Rest sounds nice," he murmured against Morpheus' lips. "You in my bed first sounds nicer. Let's put that thing somewhere safe, and maybe we can tire each other out in a more pleasurable way."

Morpheus watched with hooded eyes as Hugh placed the jar in a cabinet, safely out of the way of curious felines. With that task complete, he allowed himself to be drawn further into the cottage, toward Hugh's bedroom.

SEVEN

HUGH COULDN'T HELP the unconscious easing of tension in his shoulders as he, Morpheus, and Mary Walthorpe rode along the well-trodden fox hunting trails crisscrossing Idlebride Estate, the Walthorpe's family seat.

Mary, kitted out in a black hunt jacket and old-fashioned jodhpurs flared loosely at the hips, was mounted on a steady little piebald cob. Her advanced age was balanced by the eighty-odd years she'd presumably spent in the saddle, and she'd seemed to take it as a point of pride that she was still able to mount from the ground unassisted.

"The day I can't mount a fifteen-hand horse is the day they put me in the ground," she'd said, waving away Hugh's offer of assistance with a smile.

Hugh's body never quite seemed to forget how to sit a horse, no matter how many decades passed between rides. He'd been given the raw-boned, ten-year-old gelding whose cracked hoof he'd patched during his last farrier visit. The animal was huge and easy tempered, with a soft mouth and a compliant nature. Within minutes, Hugh felt as though he'd come home—the echo of the man he'd been centuries ago melding seamlessly with the present.

As they passed through the vibrant green of old-growth woods, he repeatedly caught himself staring at Morpheus. It was his lover who'd secured them this invitation in the first place, with his obvious breadth of knowledge and appreciation for horseflesh.

Perhaps it should have come as no surprise that Morpheus in the saddle was a breathtaking work of art. He was a god, after all—and the ancient Greeks had possessed a particular passion for horsemanship.

Morpheus had clothed himself in modern riding attire, but he wore it as though it was the finery of a king. He sat the highly bred young mare their host had loaned him like an ancient warrior on his trusted steed, the pair moving as a single creature.

I take no responsibility if my dreams tonight are full of sexy centaurs, Hugh thought wryly.

"You did not exaggerate, madame," Morpheus said, as the mare leapt catlike over a downed log lodged partway across the trail. "She is a fine mare indeed."

Mary skirted around the obstacle on her phlegmatic little cob, and Hugh followed suit—the medieval peasant in him balking at expending unnecessary energy during travel.

"Aye, she's one of the finest we've ever produced, to my mind," Mary agreed. "I had her bred to our best stallion this spring. With luck, we'll have another just like her next year."

Hugh felt a little ember of warmth kindling in his chest at the idea of next year's crop of foals—a tangible reminder of the future, and the very hope they sought.

"A worthy goal," Morpheus replied, and Hugh pictured the repaired *pithos* nestled in his saddle bag. He willed it to capture that same spark of hope and hold it, even as he wondered how far and wide they might have to travel to fill the vessel to bursting.

Mary sobered as they entered a wider part of the trail, riding three abreast. "I must say, I wasn't certain you'd come. Not after what happened in Lower Ilham. You live quite close to the village, don't you, Hugh?"

The ember of warmth flickered, guttering.

"Yes," Hugh said. Familiar guilt flared over being here rather than lending his meager efforts to the cleanup after the recent bomb detonation. Intellectually, he understood that this work was more important—but he also knew what it must look like from the outside. For all intents and purposes, he was enjoying a nice hack in the countryside, rather than joining one of the teams removing rubble and looking for bodies.

"The loss of life was truly tragic," Morpheus said, covering for his distraction. "Hugh wished to be more involved in the recovery effort. However, the authorities are discouraging people from coming into the town unless they are formally associated with the emergency services."

That was all technically true, even if Hugh was fairly confident that he could have talked his way in if he'd tried.

"It's all quite insane, isn't it," Mary said. "One never expects such things on one's own doorstep, so to speak. Yet they appear to be happening everywhere, nowadays."

Above them, birds chirped, and insects buzzed among the tall trees. The horses' hooves clopped softly against packed dirt. No wind rustled the branches. The echoing stillness was practically an entity of its own, blanketing the scene in serenity.

"Do you never fear for the future, Mary?" Hugh asked, not certain if the question would help or harm their efforts to tease out hope from the tangle of humanity's threads.

Mary was silent for a moment, reaching down with a gnarled hand to idly straighten a hank of the cob's thick mane that had fallen on the wrong side of its neck. The animal blew out a snort and tossed its head, sending the bridle's hardware jingling.

"What would be the point?" she replied eventually. "I'm old. I won't be around to see it, either way."

"But your family," Hugh said, unable to let it go. He cut a quick glance toward Morpheus, checking for any sign of censure, but his companion appeared interested in the answer.

Again, Mary paused thoughtfully before replying.

"I think," she said slowly, "that there's no one I would trust more to shepherd the future than the children I raised on this estate, and their children, and their children's children."

Hugh thought of kind, straightforward George, and the other grandchildren he'd met during his visits to Idlebride over the years. He had no doubt that any one of them would fall to Phobetor's powers if confronted directly. But might they escape somehow, tucked away out here in the country, surrounded by the old woods and green pastures of the family's ancestral home?

Was that possibility a form of hope, in and of itself?

"You believe things will get better, then?" he asked.

Mary shrugged, her spine straight and proud in the saddle despite her advanced years. "The world runs in cycles. It always has."

"But people weren't randomly setting off bombs in innocent villages before," Hugh protested, still cut to the quick by what had happened in Lower Ilham.

Mary shot him a wry look. "Oh, I assure you. They *were*. It was just that the last time it happened here, they were Germans."

Hugh jolted in place, struck by how quickly he could forget the truth of such things. He'd been there... and yet, somehow, his mind had smoothed out the sharp edges of the past to make it a less threatening and horrific place.

"Who knows what the future will look like?" Mary mused. "But there will still *be* a future, regardless of whether humans manage to wipe themselves off the face of the planet."

"Interesting," Morpheus said. He'd been content to let the conversation unfold, but now, his sharp gaze settled on Mary's wizened features. "You seem willing to entertain the possibility of a future where everything you ever worked for is lost, and yet the prospect does not frighten you?"

Mary made a considering noise.

"Well, I hope that doesn't become the case, obviously, young man—for the sake of you and your loved ones, as well as mine." She glanced between him and Hugh with a knowing smile. "But in the end, all I have any say over is my own behavior — and to a much smaller extent, my family's behavior. If enough people refuse to succumb to fear, then I imagine the future will be just fine."

The ember in Hugh's chest began to glow again at the reminder that there must be countless other people in the world with outlooks like Mary's. Countless other places where hope still lingered.

As though reading his thoughts, Mary smiled sheepishly. "After all, if I can see the bright side of things, so can a lot of other folks. I'm nothing special, you know."

"No, you really are," Hugh disagreed, reaching down to scratch the bay gelding's withers. "You may be right about a lot of things, Mary — but you're dead wrong about that part."

❖

For the rest of the ride, Hugh led the conversation toward happier topics — the other mares that were due to foal next year, the upcoming regional dog trials, Mary's newest great-grandchild. He kept a subtle eye on Morpheus the whole time, hoping for a clue about whether he could sense anything from the clay jar he was carrying, but his companion's expression remained smooth as marble and not half so expressive.

After thanking their host for the lovely afternoon, and promising to contact her with a list of other farriers since he would once more be unavailable, Hugh excused them both so they could take their leave.

Mary hadn't remarked once about Morpheus' odd insistence on bringing his own saddlebags on a simple hour-long hack—one of which was bulging with an oddly shaped mystery object. It could have been innate British politeness in action, but Hugh suspected it had more to do with the subtle influence of a god's powers.

Once they were back in Hugh's van, pulling onto the main road, Hugh could no longer contain himself. "Well?" he demanded. "Did it work?"

Morpheus frowned, reaching into the leather satchel and retrieving the repaired clay jar. He held it up to the light streaming through the windshield, twisting it to and fro as he gazed at it intently.

"No," he said at length. "I fear it did not. I can detect no trace of power within the vessel."

Hugh tapped the steering wheel pensively. The revelation should have been devastating, by any rational measure. And yet, he couldn't help his increasing belief that this was the way forward. The spark of warmth in his chest hadn't dimmed. If anything, his enthusiasm to keep trying had only grown.

"I think that might have been my fault," he said. "I shouldn't have brought up the bad things that are happening. Mary is wonderful, but she's only one person. What if we're thinking too small?"

Morpheus gave Hugh his full attention. "What do you mean?"

"Exactly what I said," Hugh replied. "Don't give up on this yet, okay? Let's think bigger. I'll do some research when we get back to the cottage, because if one person wasn't enough to move the needle, it only means we need to find larger concentrations of hope, that's all."

EIGHT

FOR THE NEXT stage of the plan—if it could really be called that—Hugh ended up dusting off his passport with its highly misleading date of birth and painfully unflattering photo. He'd been stymied at first, when it came to locating large concentrations of human hope—his brain frozen with indecision and uncertainty.

Once again, the internet had broken the proverbial log jam. As much as he hated to admit it, the thing was proving its usefulness in a number of different ways since he'd given in and joined the twenty-first century.

He and Morpheus had started in the western United States, at the edge of the Mojave Desert, not far from the playboys' playground of Las Vegas. There, a co-op of ranchers was running a desert reclamation project, using cattle to reseed areas that had once been grassland before turning to bare sand and thorny shrubs as decades of overgrazing took their toll.

Hugh had posed as a reporter for a specialist online agricultural publication in the UK. The project leaders had been downright enthusiastic about giving him and his taciturn 'assistant' the full tour by helicopter.

It was fascinating stuff in its own right. The ranchers were hauling in huge, cylindrical one-ton bales of specially grown hay, harvested when the heat- and drought-resistant grass species had already gone to seed, and using tractors to spread the bales on the sandy ground like a thick carpet.

A massive herd of desert-bred longhorn cattle followed, hemmed in by movable electric fences that confined them to a tightly controlled section of land for a brief period—usually twelve hours. During that time, the mob of hungry cattle ate about half of the hay and trampled the other half into the ground, fertilizing it with their own waste in the heavily trafficked area.

Then the next fenced section was set up adjacent to the current one, a gate in the dividing fence was opened, and the hungry herd moved onto their next twelve-hour feast of hay. Water was hauled in daily by tanker truck, and cowhands on horseback or ATV watched over the herd at all times to head off any escape attempts and deter predators.

On the surface, it sounded like an expensive and wasteful—not to mention, inconvenient—way to raise beef cattle. But the view from the air told the full story. Over the headsets, their unofficial tour guide pointed out the patchwork grid of varying shades of green contrasting with the dull reddish-brown of the desert.

Where the cattle had been, grass was sprouting from the trampled hay seeds and fertilizing cow patties. Some squares were the pale, yellow green of tender new growth. Others were the darker, more verdant hue of established pasture.

"Are you irrigating this land?" Hugh had asked, fascinated.

"No," their guide had replied. "That's the beauty of it. Much of the desert out here used to be grassland. In fact, there are studies in Africa showing that if you revegetate large enough areas, the weather patterns start to change around them. Cooler temperatures, more rainfall. It was the loss of the bison herds that caused the loss of the grasslands in this part of the world. We can reverse that process using other grazing animals. We just need to replicate the way the buffalo swept through one area on their way to the next, mowing and fertilizing the plants as they went."

The entire operation was run by only a couple dozen people, but to Hugh, the air of hope surrounding the project was palpable. The entire time, Morpheus held the pair's 'camera bag' close, with Elpis' repaired jar nestling safely inside.

From Nevada, they traveled back across the ocean to Tel Aviv. Or, rather, *Hugh* flew to Tel Aviv, and Morpheus appeared at his side as he left the airport. A rented car took them southwest through Israel, to a small village located roughly halfway between the bustling city and the town of Bethlehem.

The signs of war and destruction lay all around them, embodied not only in the blast damage to buildings and infrastructure, but also in the hard-faced men and women dressed in military fatigues and holding rifles at the ready.

Their destination, the village known as Wahat Al-Salam in Arabic and Neve Shalom in Hebrew, had not escaped the madness completely unscathed. But here, there were no armed and uniformed guards walking around. Civilians strolled through the central business district, many with children in tow.

The Oasis of Peace was a fifty-year-old social experiment, founded by an Egyptian Jew who'd fled the Nazi invasion of France and later become a Dominican Priest. Here, a roughly equal number of Jewish and Palestinian households lived intermingled, engaging in a local governmental process based on open communication and radical acceptance.

It had taken some digging on Hugh's part to come up with a contact who could get them invited to the village—but once they arrived, Morpheus' flawless linguistic prowess with both Hebrew and Arabic smoothed their way considerably.

Several of the local officials also spoke English, and before long they had a tour of the village school, where Jewish and Palestinian children received bilingual education side by side. A tour of the Pluralistic Spiritual Center where social events and meetings were held followed, and they stopped in at several of the village businesses to 'interview' the owners and patrons afterward.

Again, Hugh was struck by the lightening of the heavy weight in his chest, at this reminder of humanity's ability to look past fear and conflict in favor of striving for a better future. By contrast, Morpheus looked drawn and pale as he took his leave afterward for the Night Lands.

Hugh knew the God of Dreams was seeing to his own duties in addition to accompanying him on their jaunts in the Sublunary. Yet it still worried him that Morpheus didn't seem to feel the same sense of hope as Hugh.

Finally, after a trip to sub-Saharan Africa and a commune of women who'd banded together to start a dairy co-op for the milk produced by their goats, Hugh confronted his lover as they stood in the darkness at the edge of the small collection of huts.

"Wait, don't disappear yet," he said, taking Morpheus by the arm and turning him so they faced each other. "There's obviously something wrong. I need you to talk to me, all right?"

Morpheus remained tense in Hugh's grip for a moment, but then he sighed heavily.

"Yes. Forgive me," he said, and let the rucksack he was carrying slide down from his shoulder. He reached inside, pulling out the clay jar hidden there.

They both stared at the *pithos* with its thin web of sparkling opal veins.

"You don't mean…" Hugh began hesitantly.

"I can sense no hint of power trapped within the jar," Morpheus said, his tone flat. "There is no indication that being in the physical proximity of human hope is affecting my sister's vessel in any way."

Hugh's gaze shot up to capture his companion's in the moonlight. Strange birds called from the scrubby trees dotting the unseen savannah. Insects buzzed.

"That can't be right," he said stupidly. If *he* could feel the aura of hope surrounding them as though it was a nearly physical force, surely the pithos could feel it, too. Surely it could recognize the same force that had spilled from its shattered body inside a long-ago Greek villa.

"The presence of a god's essence is quite unmistakable," Morpheus said, still in that dead tone of hopelessness.

"To another god, you mean?" Hugh asked, since he'd sensed nothing out of the ordinary from the smaller opal necklace Morpheus had gifted Iridaceae. That necklace had contained a tiny portion of his own deific power, yet it had seemed quite unremarkable to Hugh's human senses. "Are you sure it isn't because we haven't fed enough into it yet? Could there be, I don't know, a sort of minimum threshold for you to feel it, or something?"

"I am quite certain, Hugh," Morpheus replied, with careful patience. "The vessel is inert. It remains empty."

Hugh hesitated, aware that this news was devastating. Yet, somehow it couldn't entirely dispel the buzz of excitement that had settled in his bones over the hectic week of world travel.

"All right," he said, fingers squeezing around the wiry bicep he still held. "We'll just have to go back to the drawing board, then, won't we? If nothing else, we've established that your sister's gift is still floating around in the mortal realm."

Morpheus frowned, a small furrow forming between his brows. "Have we established that?"

Hugh frowned back at him. "Well... *yes*. It seems clear as day to me. Did you not feel it as well?"

The God of Dreams opened his mouth, paused, and closed it. After a slight hesitation, he tried again. "While I can certainly see that some groups of humans are still attempting to work in harmony for the future, I would not say that I am aware of the presence of hope as an independent entity. Not in the way I am aware of, for instance, the presence of the collective unconscious."

"Really?" Hugh asked, taken aback.

Morpheus tilted his chin, imbuing the movement with the same feel as a shrug. Abruptly, Hugh was hit with the realization that they were going to need to approach this from a different direction entirely. After all the effort that had gone into procuring the *pithos* and traveling halfway across the world, it was a bit of a blow.

It did not, however, change the fact that Hugh could *feel* Elpis' power in the places they'd visited, even if Morpheus couldn't.

"Well… it sounds like we need a new angle," he said, purposely keeping his tone upbeat. "Or maybe a new set of eyes?" He tapped the outside of his thigh with restless fingers, thinking. "Who else could we approach as a potential ally? There were *loads* of gods in the old Greek myths. Surely not everyone in the Night Lands is as thrilled about Phobetor's meddling as Phantasos seems to be?"

Morpheus' marble features went through a series of small, but surprisingly wide-ranging emotions — the planes of his face luminous in the moonlight.

"I suppose… there might be one such person," he said eventually, as though the words were being pulled from him. "However, reaching him will not be simple. He closed off his realm millennia ago."

Hugh gave Morpheus' arm a small squeeze and let him go. "It's still worth a try, though, isn't it? So, tell me. Who is this mysterious divine hermit?"

NINE

"DIONYSUS?" IRIDACEAE asked, with understandable skepticism. "Seriously? I thought you hated his guts."

Morpheus and Hugh had returned to England, hoping to regroup after the fiasco involving the complete inability of his sister's repaired pithos to perform the function for which it had been designed. They were no closer to a solution than when they had started down this path, and while they'd been wasting time, the widespread madness in the Sublunary had continued to march forward with relentless inevitability.

Morpheus could not understand Hugh's continued optimism in the face of their complete failure to achieve any of their goals. However, as much as the idea of crawling to his distant cousin for help irked him, he could acknowledge that seeking allies against Phobetor was sound strategy.

"Dionysus is… not prone to serious discussion on any subject," Morpheus replied, with as much tact as he could manage.

"What, is he drunk all the time or something?" Hugh asked, pausing to stroke Baphometh as the cat hopped onto his lap and meowed for attention. He looked mildly confused by the small creature's sudden affection toward him.

Morpheus knew that his own expression had turned as sour as the grapes in the God of Wine's vineyards. "Generally, yes. That is, when he's not too busy dancing, having sex with one or more partners, or engaging in gluttony."

"I once saw him doing all four of those things at once," Iridaceae said conversationally. "There was a goat involved. It was a bit distressing, actually."

Hugh opened his mouth, thought better of whatever he was about to say, and closed it again.

"My cousin blocked off his realm in the Night Lands long ago," Morpheus said, redirecting the conversation to more practical considerations. "Once his cult died down and people moved on to different gods, he lost interest in the mortal world."

Hugh frowned. "So… can you break in to see him or something? Or at least get a message to him? I thought your lot couldn't really do that if the owner of the realm in question wanted to keep you out."

"In general, that is the case," Morpheus admitted. Both Phobetor and Phantasos had closed their realms to him when the conflict between them had come to a head. It was the reason he'd been forced to enter the borderland of Hallucination via the mortal realm to rescue Hugh from his brothers' clutches. "However, I do not propose to break in."

Both Hugh and Iridaceae looked suddenly suspicious.

"Oh?" Hugh said. "Then what exactly *are* you proposing?"

Morpheus sighed. "Just because faith in the old gods has waned, it doesn't mean the Cult of Dionysus has died out completely. Those that remain have lost portions of the sacred knowledge over the millennia. But if someone were to give them back that knowledge…"

Hugh tilted his head thoughtfully. "Someone like a different god, for instance?"

"Precisely," Morpheus said, with all the enthusiasm he felt at the prospect. Which was to say, none at all. "I am confident that if someone in the Sublunary performed the Dionysian Mysteries correctly after such a long time, it would draw my cousin's curiosity. He is, at heart, the embodiment of self-centeredness, after all."

"Hedonism incarnate," Hugh muttered. "I bet he's loads of fun at parties."

"He *invented* parties," Morpheus said flatly.

Iridaceae leaned an elbow on the table and rested her chin on her hand. "This isn't going to involve you becoming mortal and taking a bunch of weird drugs again, is it? Because I still haven't recovered from the last time."

Baphometh trilled agreement, and Hugh shot Morpheus a look that said it had damned well *better not* involve those things.

"No," Morpheus said. "It will not. Instead, it will involve *Hugh* ingesting a very specific set of mind-altering substances. And probably quite a lot of wine."

"Well… I suppose it won't be the first time," Hugh grumbled. "On either count."

"Also, there are bees involved," Morpheus said. The others looked at him incredulously.

"No offense, but your family is whacked," Hugh said after a pause. "You do know that, right?"

"I am aware," Morpheus said stiffly.

Once again, Hugh was able to use his *world wide web* to find the nearest concentration of practicing pagan Hellenists. This happened to be a group of about two dozen individuals who gathered fortnightly on privately owned land north of Maidstone, near the site of a small stone circle from the megalithic period.

The estate boasted, among many other things, a thriving vineyard. Morpheus had nodded his agreement when Hugh suggested contacting the eccentric owner.

"Sounds like it's pretty much purpose-built for summoning a god who likes wine," Hugh had observed, and immediately started typing out an *e-mail*.

Morpheus used the time while they communicated back and forth to gather the herbs utilized in his cousin's preferred rituals. Some species had died out in the mortal realm, and now existed only in the Night Lands. Others, like milk of the poppy, could be found in both places.

Eventually, Hugh relayed that he'd successfully set up a meeting in person with the owner of the estate, who also happened to lead the quasi-religious pagan group.

"You realize how crazy we're going to sound," Hugh warned. "Just because this bloke is eccentric, it doesn't mean he's automatically going to believe in Greek gods being real and the world being about to end."

"That will not be a concern," Morpheus told him.

Hugh shot him a side-eyed glance. "You're about to throw the whole *'gods can't interfere in the mortal realm'* thing completely out the window, aren't you."

Morpheus held his gaze. "If we are to fight a war, doing so with one arm tied back seems the height of foolishness, would you not agree?"

"Oh, believe me. That wasn't a complaint," Hugh said. "It's all just starting to feel a lot more real than when we were traipsing around the globe looking at interesting social projects."

Somehow, Morpheus couldn't argue the sentiment.

Leaving Iridaceae behind once more with the cat she'd become so inexplicably fond of, Morpheus checked in on his own realm while Hugh drove the fifty miles or so from his cottage to the Vixen's Coty estate and winery in Kent. Assured that nothing alarming had happened to his kingdom in his absence, he focused on the familiar mind of his human lover and stepped through the veil, reappearing in the passenger seat of the rattling van.

"*Balls!*" Hugh flinched violently, then caught himself and dragged his attention back to the road. "You should've saved that trick for Sir Reginald Cardsley. It might get his attention, if nothing else."

"Such theatrics will not be necessary," Morpheus said.

They pulled onto the drive leading up to the large manor house. Hugh parked on the well-kept gravel near the towering front doors, and they were

shown in politely by an elderly man in an impecca-
ble black suit.

Their host—not much younger than his servant,
but dressed far less formally—entered the pleasant
drawing room where they'd been seated. Morpheus
rose.

"You are Sir Reginald Cardsley?" he asked
without preamble. "Good. There is a matter of some
urgency that we must discuss with you." As Hugh
stepped forward to exchange tiresome pleasantries,
Morpheus reached out, finding the shape of their
host's consciousness, and said, "*Come with me.*"

His voice resonated with power.

Morpheus was only vaguely aware of Hugh
catching the man's limp body as he shepherded Sir
Reginald into a lucid dream state. A few minutes
later, having relayed the relevant information directly to the man's mind, Morpheus returned his
focus fully to the Sublunary. He found Hugh bracing the shoulders of the snoring Sir Reginald to keep
him from tumbling forward out of his chair.

"Bit more warning next time, love?" Hugh said
plaintively.

"Forgive me," Morpheus told him. "I thought
efficiency was of the essence."

He snapped his fingers, and Sir Reginald
gasped awake. Hugh immediately let go of the old
man's shoulders and stepped away, giving him
space.

The human's gaze snapped back and forth between them several times. His watery brown eyes
were as round as dinner plates.

"I say!" he exclaimed. "Was I asleep just now? And… is all of this true?"

"The world is ending, and we need you to help us call an ancient god out of retirement so he can help stop it?" Hugh asked. "Yeah, 'fraid so, mate. What do you say?"

Sir Reginald still looked like his eyes were in danger of popping straight out of his skull. "This is extraordinary! You are the *actual God of Dreams*?" His startled gaze moved to Hugh. "And you are the Eternal Hunter of legend?"

Hugh shot Morpheus an unimpressed glance. "That second part is a bit complicated, I'm afraid. He's definitely the God of Dreams, though. So, how about it? Are you up for hosting a good, old-fashioned bacchanalia? Because we're kind of on a schedule here."

Sir Reginald's eyes lit up like a child offered the keys to the toymaker's factory. He looked between them again, rubbing his wrinkled hands together in apparent glee.

"Oh, I've been waiting for this moment my *entire life*," he said. "Stay here, the both of you. I need to make some phone calls."

TEN

AND THAT WAS HOW Hugh found himself in the middle of a cut-rate stone circle at the edge of a vineyard, holding narcotic-laced wine in a massive cup carved from a bull's horn, and watching nervously as hundreds of bees swarmed around a shallow bowl of sugar water nearby.

He had to give his fellow revelers this much, at least—they were an enthusiastic bunch.

"I say, Reggie!" exclaimed a reed-thin fellow who could have convincingly portrayed one of the contestants in the Monty Python 'upper-class twit of the year' skit that Iridaceae had showed him on YouTube a few days ago. "This is brilliant! Why have we never done the Dionysian Mysteries before?"

A short, curvy, middle-aged woman stood nearby, eyeing the buzzing excitement around the bowl. "Because of the bees, I'm guessing? Seriously, Reg—are you one hundred percent certain no one here is allergic? Because that's a lawsuit waiting to happen."

Sir Reginald cleared his throat. "Well, it was either the bees or a sacrificial goat. And you know how faint I get at the sight of blood."

"Don't be such a *solicitor*, Gwen," said a younger man who'd come dressed in an honest-to-god toga.

Hugh hadn't had the heart to point out that togas were from the Roman era, not the Greek one. On the other hand, there was functionally very little difference between the Greek Dionysus and the Roman Bacchus. They were, presumably, the same bloke.

"Now, enough chit chat!" Sir Reginald exclaimed, clapping his hands together. "Musicians, are you ready? Once our friend here, our *sacred vessel*, has taken a good, deep draught from his, er... vessel—"

"The bull's-horn goblet is called a *kantharos*," Morpheus said, with careful patience.

"Yes, of course. Once he has drunk from his *kantharos*, he will take up this staff thingie..." Sir Reginald held up a rod decorated with ivy and topped with a large pine cone.

"The *thyrsus*," Morpheus corrected in a monotone.

"Er, of course. What he said." Sir Reginald cleared his throat. "At that point, the dancing will commence, continuing until the great god Dionysus travels down to our realm to possess the sacred vessel, that he may grant us his largesse."

By 'sacred vessel,' he meant Hugh, of course. Also, a quick glance at Morpheus confirmed that largesse was likely to be thin on the ground, after dragging the God of Hedonism out of his self-imposed solitude so that his distant cousin could try to guilt-trip him into joining a war.

Hugh had done a lot of crazy shit over the course of his unnaturally long life, but getting possessed by a deity was going to be a new one, even for him. Assuming it worked, of course.

"Right," he said, without enthusiasm. "Here we go, then. What exactly did you say was in this wine?"

"Several obscure herbs, the names of which wouldn't mean much to you. And also, a fair amount of raw opium." Morpheus paused. "I will remind you that this quest to parlay with my cousin was originally your idea."

"I remember," Hugh said sourly. He heaved a gusty sigh. "Well, it's not like I can die of it." With that, he tipped up the carved bull's-horn goblet and let the contents slide into his mouth.

He wasn't certain what he'd expected, exactly— but he definitely hadn't expected it to be the best thing he'd ever drunk. Whatever psychotropic substances were floating around in the full-bodied red, they also happened to taste *amazing*.

That at least made it easier to square his shoulders and start chugging, anyway. Immediately, a raucous chant of "Drink… drink… drink… *drink!*" that wouldn't have been out of place at a Fresher's Week bash filled the air. It devolved into cheers and shouts of approval when Hugh tipped the horn up to swallow the last dregs and held it aloft in triumph.

He raised an eyebrow at Morpheus once the cheers died down. "You know, if the whole 'saving humanity' thing goes tits up, you could always make a fortune selling this stuff by the bottle. It's pretty brill."

His lover's lips pressed together. "Hmm. You shouldn't be surprised at the taste, given the origins of the recipe. However, I'm not certain that drinkers would appreciate being randomly possessed by a god after imbibing."

"Good point," Hugh said.

Sir Reginald approached, the ivy-decorated rod resting on his outstretched palms. "Your thryce... your thurz..." He stumbled over the unfamiliar word and coughed to cover it. "Your staff, good sir."

Hugh reached for the *thyrsus*, surprised when his hands nearly overshot the mark. After a bit of fumbling, the transfer was successfully achieved. Nearby — albeit somewhat farther removed from the bees — the musicians struck up a jaunty tune with a drum, pan flute, and some kind of long, straight, antique-looking trumpet.

Given the general air of cheerful incompetence among the group, it was actually quite catchy. Hugh, who'd had to cultivate a basic background in dance to meet societal expectations over the centuries, found his body swaying in the unconscious way of someone dancing alone in their kitchen to the sound of a favorite song.

Around him, the other members of the self-styled *Society of Ageless Pagans* — who had presumably never noticed that their acronym was *S.O.A.P.* — began to jump in as well, with widely varying degrees of grace and rhythm.

A lovely, warm feeling of comradery began to bubble up in Hugh's chest, displacing the constant worry and stress that had wrapped around his ribcage for what seemed like the last century or so, at the very least. He swayed toward Morpheus, wanting to draw him into the happy cluster of laughing and dancing.

"Dance with me!" he said, reaching out the hand that wasn't clasping the ridiculous staff.

To his surprise, Morpheus took his offered hand, lifting it to press a kiss to the knuckles before drawing him into a gentle spin. "My hunter," he said, his low voice pitched for Hugh's ears alone. "Revelry suits you. I see I shall have to watch you carefully within my cousin's realm."

The world didn't stop spinning when Hugh did, but somehow it didn't matter. Cool hands directed Hugh's movements, just enough to keep him upright and dancing. The cloudy, rain-damp field at the edge of the vineyard began to sparkle in Hugh's vision. The bees became tiny drops of molten gold, suspended around the brightly painted bowl of sugar water. The grass was the deepest shade of emerald he'd ever seen. His fellow dancers glowed from within. The notes of the impromptu band hung in the air, each one twinkling joyously for a few instants before fading away.

Morpheus was all shadows among the brilliance of the dance—involved, but apart. Hugh wanted to kiss him... wondered if he'd allow it.

"Of course I would," Morpheus said. Then he lifted his voice from its intimate murmur. "May we have the bullroarer now, please?"

Hugh blinked, colored afterimages weaving across his vision like streamers as he tried to place the words in context. Then, a new sound joined the drum and other instruments. It was rhythmic, but unlike anything Hugh had heard before. As much vibration as sound, it rumbled through his chest like a low-frequency earthquake.

Abruptly, he was aware of the eerie sound moving through him… as though his body was a conduit, directing the deep noise to someplace unseen and otherwise unreachable. He stumbled. Cool hands caught him, but not before he was surrounded by the swarm of buzzing bees. Instinct urged him to swat wildly at the insects, but gentle hands encircled his wrists, preventing him from flailing.

"Easy," said Morpheus' rough-velvet voice. "They are in a trance, much as you are. They will relay events to my cousin's realm, but they will not harm you. Now, my hunter—let us facilitate this meeting."

Morpheus transferred both of Hugh's wrists to one hand, before raising his other hand and resting his palm on Hugh's forehead. It felt lovely, and Hugh momentarily forgot about the bees in favor of pressing into it.

In the next moment, Morpheus used the point of contact to flick Hugh's head sharply backward, like a fundamentalist preacher calling forth the Holy Spirit at a church meeting in the American South. Hugh's body felt like it was falling backward… except it *wasn't* his body. It was something else. His soul?

The experience felt oddly circular, as though he somehow fell so far that he slammed right back into his physical form. Except… something infinitely larger and stronger than he was caught him before he could settle back into place.

"Well," rumbled a deep mental voice in a tone of amusement. "I have to say, I certainly wasn't expecting *this*."

ELEVEN

MORPHEUS LIFTED HIS chin and consciously un-clenched his jaw, pushing his dislike of seeing another god possessing his lover's body to one side with difficulty.

"Cousin," he greeted. "Thank you for coming. I could think of no other way to draw you from your realm, since you locked the rest of us away from it."

Hugh's head cocked. The personality shining from behind his earthy brown eyes was not his own.

"Morpheus." Hugh's vocal cords struggled to produce the old familiar, booming voice. "I certainly didn't expect to find *you* cavorting with human revelers. You're looking very, er, *well*."

Only Dionysus could make a completely innocuous word sound so salacious.

The God of Revelry turned, taking in the crowd of increasingly drunken dancers. "I do like your new friends!"

The Society of Ageless Pagans cheered as one, throwing their hands in the air. Dionysus lifted Hugh's arm, giving an enthusiastic whoop in return and shaking his ceremonial staff in solidarity.

Sir Reginald crept forward cautiously, dropping to one knee and bowing his head low. "Is it true? Are you really the great god Dionysus, come to Earth to possess your sacred vessel and share your great wisdom with us lowly mortals?"

Morpheus drew breath, intent on pointing out that they'd already *had* a god in their midst, thank you very much—but Dionysus beat him to it.

"Yup, that's me. And, hey, why not?" Hugh's features frowned down at the prostrate nobleman. "The first piece of wisdom is this. Stop bowing and scraping. Get up and have a drink, already! You people aren't *nearly* drunk enough yet. Also, why isn't anyone fucking? This is supposed to be an orgy!"

He raised the staff again, and the cheering grew uproarious. Someone handed Sir Reginald a goblet and helped him to his feet, red liquid splashing over the brim as he staggered upright. Nearby, the woman who'd been concerned about legal liability if someone got stung by a bee turned and tackled the scrawny young man wearing a historically inaccurate toga. A second later, the two were tangled on the ground, kissing each other with more enthusiasm than skill.

More wine-filled goblets magically appeared. They were passed around, and the musicians started up again. The tune this time was primal, with a deep, throbbing drumbeat. The dancing grew vastly less coherent and vastly more suggestive.

"That's better!" Dionysus called out approvingly. "Now, who brought a goat? Anyone?"

Morpheus sighed, grasping Hugh's arm and bringing Dionysus' attention back to him.

"*Cousin*," he said, more firmly this time. "We have much to discuss. As lovely as this bacchanalia may be, if you wish for there to be similar gatherings in the future, we must first address my brother Phobetor's ill-advised intervention in the Sublunary."

Dionysus stilled, finally looking at Morpheus properly. Coming through his lover's eyes as it did, the regard was oddly disconcerting.

"Phobetor? What's that little stick insect gone and done now?" His gaze turned inward for a moment, as though he were rifling through Hugh's mind for the relevant information. "*Oh*. Well, that was certainly idiotic of him. What a prat. It's true that rules are made to be broken, but what's the point of trashing the whole of creation like a toddler throwing toys out of the crib?"

Morpheus' teeth ground together in response to the casual invasion of Hugh's mind, but he kept his voice level as he replied. "Perhaps we might continue this discussion in your realm? And preferably, in separate bodies."

Dionysus sighed. "Oh, very well. If you insist." He glanced around at the revelers. While they'd been speaking, the dance had devolved into a pile of writhing bodies, rife with moans and groans of ecstasy. "It appears my work here is done, anyway."

"Quite so," Morpheus replied stiffly.

Dionysus ran Hugh's hands down his body in a suggestive manner.

"I *do* approve of your new human, by the way," he said. "He seems very interesting. Wouldn't have thought he'd be your type."

Morpheus bristled. "If we might depart?" The words emerged clipped.

Dionysus laughed. "Aww, I've never seen you like this before, cousin. All right, then. Let's go. This group gets points for enthusiasm, but I daresay I can provide much better hospitality back home."

An instant later, Morpheus felt a strong tug as he and Hugh were pulled through the veil separating the mortal realm from the Night Lands; and again as Dionysus slipped them past the defenses surrounding his private kingdom.

They reappeared in a gilded banquet hall. Hugh was dressed in a scandalously short and revealing Greek *exomis*, the crimson fabric hanging off one shoulder, and the bottom of the belted tunic barely long enough to preserve his modesty. Morpheus glanced down at his own body, his lips quirking in irritation when he found himself similarly clad. He waved a hand down the length of his torso, brusquely replacing the purple-dyed linen with his usual—and much more modest—clothing.

Hugh, once more free of possessing gods, wavered in place before catching himself. "Whoa. Okay. That was… *different*. Also, why am I not drunk anymore? Is my body lying in a muddy field with a bunch of bees buzzing around it?"

Dionysus, now his usual bearded, bluff and hearty self, flicked his fingers. A golden goblet of mead appeared in his hand. He pressed it on Hugh, who took it helplessly.

"No, no," he said. "Your physical form is surprisingly easy to transport while I'm possessing it. And your boyfriend is being all *stern and serious*, so I figured you'd want to start the conversation sober, at least. Not that you should necessarily stay that way."

He made another gesture, and two giggling nymphs appeared, chivvying Hugh backwards to lie on a velvet-upholstered chaise placed conveniently behind him. "Erm," Hugh said, as the pair knelt next to him and began administering a sensual massage. A goat wandered past, pausing to bleat at them before wandering off.

Morpheus shot Hugh a questioning glance. The human gave a bewildered shrug in reply—confused, but not appearing alarmed or openly distressed. Elsewhere in the echoing room, music started up—the unearthly strains of a harp in expert hands, accompanied by a light and soulful male voice.

Dionysus gestured to a second low couch across from Hugh's chaise. He settled himself on a third, facing them both. As though an invisible signal had been given, two satyrs hurried over and began rubbing themselves lasciviously against Dionysus, kissing each other with passionate fervor a scant few inches above his lap.

Morpheus sighed again, although he did at least attempt to do so silently. He remained standing, having no wish to succumb to the hedonism on display all around him.

"Look," Hugh began, trying manfully to ignore the two nymphs currently giving him a foot massage. "This is all very… nice. But we really do need to talk to you about what's happening in the human realm. Morpheus says you, um, don't get out much—"

Morpheus was unable to stifle a soft snort of derision.

" —so, you may not be aware of how bad things are," Hugh concluded.

"My sister died after giving up her immortality to live with a human lover," Morpheus said, plowing ahead. "Her gift of hope was squandered; spread to the four winds by a jealous and short-sighted mortal. Its loss unbalanced the Sublunary. Possibly the Night Lands as well. More recently, Phobetor orchestrated my own capture by mortals. I was held for eighty years, and dreams weakened as a result. My brother took advantage of the cosmic imbalance to seize control in the human realm."

"We're killing each other," Hugh added quietly. "And since you've been gone, we've developed the weapons to do so on a massive scale."

Dionysus sobered. "When you say 'massive'…"

"They could destroy all life on the planet with the press of a button," Morpheus said.

Hugh looked ill. "Christ. When you put it like that…"

The human glanced down at the goblet in his hands, then raised it to his lips and tipped it back, clearly ready to be drunk again.

Dionysus shot Hugh a sour glance. "I'll thank you not to speak that usurper's name inside my palace. Nevertheless, I can understand your predicament."

Hugh set the goblet aside and wiped his lips with the back of his hand, still valiantly attempting not to react to the nymphs. "We need allies," he said. "We're hoping you might be one."

Dionysus grunted, stroking blunt fingers through the hair of the nearest satyr. "I gave up on humanity long ago. They've forgotten the old ways. Forgotten *us*."

Hugh sat forward, suddenly intent. "And yet, one little ceremony and you couldn't get down there fast enough."

Morpheus raised an eyebrow and let Hugh take point in the conversation, aware of just how effectively his lover could cut through a god's obfuscation.

Indeed, Dionysus appeared discomfited in response to the verbal sally. "Well, I won't deny a sense of curiosity. It's been a very long time since anyone bothered with the proper trappings. Even if you *did* forget the goat." He shot Morpheus a flat stare. "Should've known someone was reading the lines to the actors from behind the scenes."

"You could teach them how to do it again, you know," Hugh argued. "Humans love that kind of shit. Seriously. Drinking? Orgies? Gluttony? That's a winning proposition. It's not their fault they forgot how to do it to your exacting specifications. I mean, Morpheus says some of the herbs and stuff aren't even *available* in the mortal realm anymore. But you could fix that, right?"

Dionysus' expression turned calculating. "Humans have moved on from the old gods."

Hugh didn't back down. "Mate, the God of Fear is literally trying to *rule the world*. I think you'll find that your lot has never been more relevant than they are *right the fuck now*."

Dionysus threw his head back and laughed. "Little mortal, how in Eros' name did you end up screwing my prissy killjoy of a cousin?"

"Not technically mortal, and just lucky, I guess," Hugh said, without missing a beat.

Dionysus snorted in amusement. "You could do better. You should dump him and come be my consort instead." He leaned back, spreading his arms along the back of the low divan. "Tell you what. You two spend the night here, and match me drink for drink. Do that, and in the morning, I'll give you the option of staying here with me permanently. Let the rest of the universe tear itself apart. We'll drink and eat and fuck away the rest of eternity."

Disappointment flickered across Hugh's pleasant features. Morpheus, not one to give up so easily, moved forward to loom over Dionysus' lounging form. The satyrs scampered away, their tails stiff with alarm.

"No," Morpheus said. "However, I do have a counterproposal. We will stay and drink with you. In the morning, you may offer us permanent sanctuary if you still wish. But if we refuse, you will agree to help us stand against Phobetor and Phantasos."

Dionysus' heavy brows twitched. "Phantasos, too? Surely the lad hasn't thrown in his lot with the God of Fear."

"He has," Hugh said grimly. "The little twat kidnapped me and dragged me away to Hallucination, so Phobetor could use me as bait to draw Morpheus."

Dionysus' shoulders sagged. "Ah, damn. Not *Phantasos*. Fantasy has no business allying with fear. What was the lad *thinking*?"

"Ally with us, and you can ask him yourself," Morpheus said, giving no quarter. "Do we have a deal, cousin?"

Dionysus heaved out a breath from the depths of his generous belly.

"Very well," he agreed. "One night of drinking, and I'll see if I can sway you from this madness. But if I can't, I suppose I'll have to join you in your insanity."

"Brilliant," Hugh said faintly, eyeing his half-full goblet of divine mead.

TWELVE

IT WOULD BE inaccurate to say that Hugh was unfamiliar with nights like this one. Admittedly, staying out all night drinking with the lads in a filthy medieval tavern wasn't quite in the same league as drinking with a couple of *actual gods* inside a golden palace. Still, the principle appeared to be the same.

"To Elpis!" Dionysus boomed, lifting his goblet. "Can't say I remember her at all, but I'm sure she must've been lovely!"

"To Elpis," Hugh echoed, layering on the false enthusiasm. He raised his own cup, tilting it back and taking a moment to appreciate how much better the wine here was than the sour swill he and his mates had been able to afford in the twelve hundreds.

Morpheus was silent and grim-faced as he drained his silver chalice, his expression clearly conveying how little interest he had in playing his cousin's games.

Dionysus rolled his eyes, although Hugh thought he could detect a hint of wry fondness in the expression. He gestured between Hugh and Morpheus with the hand holding the goblet. "Seriously, I'm just not seeing the appeal here, Hugh. You seem like a man who knows how to have a good time. And I know for a fact that my cousin *doesn't*. How in the mortal world did you end up with him?"

Hugh felt his cheeks heat at the memory of some of his and Morpheus' wilder sexual escapades within the realm of dreams, and decided to blame the wine. He cleared his throat, aware of the weight of Morpheus' glacier blue gaze on him.

"In my defense," Hugh managed, "he is *unbearably* hot. I mean… just *look* at him."

The nymphs, who had at least stopped giving him a foot massage in favor of feeding each other grapes in the most suggestive way possible, giggled.

Dionysus ran a skeptical eye over the God of Dreams. "Hmm. I suppose. I mean, if you like them twinky and humorless, anyway. Ah, well. It just goes to show there's someone for everyone!"

Morpheus allowed one of the satyrs to refill his chalice, not breaking expression. "I am aware that you are trying to goad me, cousin. I am also aware that you are out of practice in conversing with anyone outside of this gilded bubble you have crafted for yourself. However, I might point out that if your goal is to get us to stay with you, insulting me is not necessarily the best way to go about it."

Hugh's attention bounced back to Dionysus, curious how the seemingly jovial god would respond to the pointed barb. He tried to ignore the way his vision seemed to lag a half-second behind the movement, aware that he was well on his way to blind drunkenness for the third time in less than a week.

Rather than being moved to anger, Dionysus appeared to sober. "Perhaps I'm trying to badger you into appreciating what you already have, free for the taking, rather than throwing yourself into a war." He tilted his head, considering. "Or perhaps I've already seen the futility of convincing you to change your course, and I'm merely attempting to lure your consort toward safe harbor. Surely you cannot wish to see him embroiled in a battle between gods, when he might remain safe and happy instead?"

Hugh drew breath to speak, fairly certain that he should have strong opinions about the topic of conversation. But he paused, the words halted by the flicker of utter devastation that peeked through Morpheus' mask of indifference for a split second.

Changing tack, Hugh pinned Dionysus with an unblinking gaze, though his words were meant as much for the God of Dreams as the God of Drink. "Yeah… we already tried that dynamic, actually. It didn't work very well. Also, no offense, but I've never really gone in for bears."

Hugh's attempt at a quelling glare slid right off Dionysus, predictably enough. Again, that look of exasperated fondness touched the god's broad features.

"All I'm hearing is, 'I'm not drunk enough yet,'" he said indulgently. "Come! More wine!"

Hugh reluctantly held out his cup, allowing the grinning satyr to fill it. It hadn't escaped his notice that the jewel encrusted vessel was perhaps one-third the size of those used by the gods. It was an interesting little nod to the idea that Dionysus wasn't actually trying to kill him via alcohol poisoning — temporary though the effect might be.

"Hugh makes his own choices," Morpheus said, after draining his own cup with deliberate, measured swallows. He still hadn't even deigned to sit down, and Hugh wondered if he could somehow will himself not to get drunk.

Hugh, who hesitantly downed his refilled cup, didn't have that option. Already, his head was starting to swim. It was the best kind of drunkenness, too. As it had in the mortal realm with the pagans, the wine dulled his awareness of all their worries, making what had been an overwhelming concern seem distant and unimportant.

When the nymphs abandoned their grapes in favor of snuggling up to him on the low chaise, it suddenly seemed like far too much effort to try and discourage them. He was peripherally aware of Morpheus and Dionysus continuing to exchange barbs. The music became upbeat... the nymphs tugged Hugh up to dance. At some point, the satyrs joined in as well.

He glanced around, trying to orient himself past his growing dizziness, and found Morpheus following his movements with a watchful, vaguely proprietary gaze. Reassured that he wasn't about to get dragged off to the land of the fae folk or something, Hugh allowed himself to be swept along in the dance.

More wine appeared at intervals. He drank it, cognizant of the rules he and Morpheus had agreed to. His arms and legs felt increasingly far away and useless, until he was only on his feet thanks to the giggling nymphs and satyrs supporting him.

When his balance finally deserted him completely, warm hands deposited him against a broad, hairy body. It was surprisingly comfortable, especially when blunt fingers started running through his hair, scratching idly over his scalp.

A terse, familiar voice cut into his awareness, the meaning of the words lost to the growing buzz inside his skull. He tried to turn toward that voice — a flower turning toward the sun — but his muscles refused to cooperate.

"Oh, just let him be." The chest he was resting against rumbled in time with the words. "He's down for the count. Don't worry, I won't hold it against our agreement for the night. He's only human, after all."

"'S a good song, that," Hugh mumbled, humming a few off-key bars of Rag'n'Bone Man, before promptly passing out.

✦

When he next awoke, he was back in his familiar bed, in his familiar bedroom, and he didn't have nearly as bad a hangover as he should have had, by rights.

"Ugh," he groaned. "Wait, was that another dream?"

"I'm afraid not," came a dry voice from nearby. "If it had been, I could have ensured it was far less tedious and irritating."

Hugh peeled open gritty eyes to find the sun filtering through his curtains, and Morpheus — appearing somewhat the worse for wear — seated on the edge of his mattress.

"How'd we get back here?" Hugh asked, trying to sort through his muddled memories with limited success. "And… please tell me that the part where I let a satyr climb me like a pole dancer is a wine-fueled hallucination?"

"Dionysus returned you here at my behest," Morpheus said, his tone carefully neutral. "As to the rest, perhaps we should leave the details to the vagaries of history."

"Right," Hugh agreed, immediately seeing the wisdom of this approach. "Um, what about the rest of it, though? Did he agree to help?"

"Somewhat surprisingly, he did." Morpheus lifted a hand as though to stroke Hugh's hair away from his face, only to halt the movement abruptly. "Forgive me, but I did refuse his other offer preemptively on your behalf. You were rather indisposed at the time."

"Thanks for that," Hugh said, relieved. "All due respect to your cousin, but I think trying to maintain that lifestyle for any length of time really *would* kill me."

Morpheus relaxed visibly, and Hugh wondered what subtext he was missing.

One dark eyebrow arched. "I am pleased to hear it. You *did* look rather comfortable in his embrace at one point."

Hugh hid a wince, more half-obscured memories bubbling queasily to the surface. "He's… well-padded? Plus, I think it might've been more a case of 'passed out' than 'comfortable'."

"Hmm." The sound was noncommittal. "And yet, I still find myself fighting the urge to remind you to whom you belong."

Hugh's dick surged—somewhat unhelpfully—with sudden interest. "Oh? Don't fight the urge on *my* account," he said.

"Perhaps later," Morpheus replied, his cool tone of promise doing nothing to alleviate Hugh's unhelpful dick situation. "But for now, you should know that my cousin has promised to visit the Titans in the Pit, in hopes of gleaning more information about Elpis and the fate of her powers."

Hugh frowned. "He did? Will the Titans even agree to speak with him? They seem a bit, erm... *temperamental* in that regard."

"They will speak to him," Morpheus replied.

"You sound very sure of that," Hugh said.

Morpheus lifted one elegant shoulder and let it drop. "He will offer them wine from his vineyards. For beings trapped in perpetual bondage, drunkenness is a far more compelling bribe than, say, a divine flame to drive back the darkness."

"Oh." Hugh considered that for a moment. "Well... yes. I suppose it would be, at that."

THIRTEEN

AFTER AGREEING TO join Hugh for a greasy, carbohydrate-laden breakfast designed to soak up the lingering remnants of alcohol and stave off the hangover that both of them so richly deserved, Morpheus excused himself and fucked off back to his realm.

Ostensibly, this was to make sure that nothing alarming had happened in his absence, and also to wait for Dionysus' report on his conversation with the Titans. However, Hugh couldn't help noticing that the dangerous glint, which had been lurking behind his lover's glacier-colored gaze ever since the awkward discussion of Hugh's drunken revels in Dionysus' realm, had yet to fade.

He had a feeling that his dreams this evening were going to be… *interesting.*

With a resigned sigh, Hugh cleared away the breakfast things and went to feed the cat. He found Baphometh curled up on a chair, his floofy tail lying neatly across his front paws and nose like a muffler.

"Aren't you hungry?" Hugh asked, shaking the bowl of kitty kibble enticingly. Baph flicked a tattered ear in his direction, but otherwise made no move to get up and eat. Hugh frowned at him, really hoping that a trip to the veterinarian in Leatherhead for his mostly feral tomcat wasn't in the cards.

"If we're doing vet bills now, you know I could always pay a bit extra and get you neutered at the same time," Hugh pointed out, receiving a half-hearted hiss in reply.

As though he'd been grievously offended, the cat roused himself and headed for the open window, disappearing outside. Hoping that the evil little fluffball had merely eaten a dodgy mouse or something, Hugh shrugged and left him to it.

In the absence of anything truly constructive to do, he spent more hours than he'd intended glued to his laptop screen, obsessively researching anything he could find on Pandora, Elpis, Epimetheus, and the concept of Hope as a universal constant. Beyond the basics available in any standard mythology textbook, the information mostly seemed pretty sus.

While Hugh had gained a new appreciation for cranks and eccentrics since becoming embroiled in Morpheus' world, most of the so-called Greek mythology gurus on the internet also seemed to be selling something. Self-help courses, aligned crystals, spiritual retreats, and so forth *probably* wouldn't help them save the world... although, given what he'd seen in recent months, Hugh couldn't rule it out entirely.

He ended up completely forgetting about lunch, and only realized how hungry he was after surfacing with bloodshot eyes and a pounding headache a few minutes before five o'clock.

"Bloody hell," he muttered to the empty living room. "So *that's* how people get addicted to the internet."

He reluctantly hauled himself up from the desk chair and went to go make food. Baphometh was nowhere to be found; the untouched bowl of kibble still sat in its corner in the boot room.

Once again, a rummage in the refrigerator and cabinets reminded Hugh that he needed to go shopping. And once again, he felt absolutely zero enthusiasm at the prospect of rushing through an ASDA filled with tense, frightened people fighting over packets of string cheese.

"Tomorrow," he promised himself, pulling out an ancient box of pasta and hoping he had something to top it with.

------------◆------------

Perhaps it was understandable that tiredness hit him almost as soon as his stomach was full. While it was true that much of last night's drunken revelry had taken place in the Night Lands, on this occasion, it hadn't been a dream. His body hadn't been safely asleep in the mortal realm, resting while he danced with satyrs and swilled divine booze.

Add to that the fact that the night spent in Dionysus' realm had been preceded by several hours spent getting pissed off his head in a muddy field, and Hugh figured he was probably owed an early night.

Baphometh had finally deigned to return, at least. He'd even eaten the sardine that Hugh pulled from his pasta as a peace offering, raising hopes that maybe a veterinarian wouldn't be needed after all. With no word yet from Morpheus, and nothing else to productively occupy his time, Hugh gave up and went to bed—viscerally conscious of the cool way Morpheus had said, "Perhaps later," when referencing whatever plans he had to assuage his uncharacteristic fit of jealousy over Hugh's drunken affections.

It didn't help that the mere prospect had Hugh hard as a rock again. Furtively — though he couldn't have said *why* he felt the need for furtiveness — Hugh worked the waistband of his pajama bottoms down over his hips and jerked himself off beneath the sheets, slow and easy. He finished into a tissue grabbed from the box on the bedside table, relishing the slow tide of warmth that rolled over him.

And if the hazy sense of possessive eyes roaming over his body was real, rather than the beginnings of a dream, it still brought the twitch of a smile to his lips.

❖

For that reason, it wasn't a complete shock when Hugh regained awareness in a familiar palace receiving hall, only to find himself naked, gagged, and shackled in a modern BDSM practitioner's idea of medieval stocks.

Hugh had actually *been* in medieval stocks — long story, don't ask — and they definitely hadn't been padded with smooth, ergonomically designed leather upholstery inside the neck and wrist holes. Nor had there been a cushioned bar to rest his hips on, with his legs splayed out in a vulnerable V-shape and cuffed to solid posts at the ankles.

There was no mistaking the grand room where Morpheus had once threatened to place Hugh out for public use by a dozen or more copies of himself. It was elegant and understated, whereas Dionysus' celebration hall had been gaudy. Rather than raucous music and dancing, Hugh was surrounded by the low hum of many sober conversations taking place at once.

The voices were all the same—a comforting, velvety resonance that was enough, these days, to turn Hugh's insides to liquid without so much as a single physical touch. He tried to crane his head from side to side, and was rewarded with peripheral glimpses of small groups of conferring figures. They were all dressed in the sort of subdued Edwardian finery that Morpheus seemed to prefer these days, when he wasn't trying to blend in on Earth.

"Bugger," Hugh tried to say around the ball gag. What emerged was two syllables of garbled nonsense.

A lull in the conversation ensued, and Hugh became aware of the weight of many gazes on him—a sense of quiet attention that prickled the fine hair on the back of his neck.

Footsteps approached. Morpheus appeared in front of him, deftly unbuckling the gag and removing it from between Hugh's teeth. Hugh worked his jaw to loosen it, peering up at the haughty figure dressed in midnight blue embroidered brocade.

"Ah," Morpheus said. "Excellent. We've been waiting for you." He stroked a cool thumb over Hugh's parted lips, dragging his lower lip down before withdrawing the touch.

Despite himself, Hugh felt a delicious shiver run down his spine and lodge firmly in his balls.

"Greet all your party guests this way, do you?" he managed.

"Hmm, no," Morpheus replied. "Only the ones in need of a reminder regarding who they belong to."

"Right," Hugh croaked, aware that anyone in the room with a decent angle would be able to see the way his dick jumped at that. "S'pose you're about to tell me that this is *my* filthy sex dream, and you're not in charge anyway."

The hint of a smile tilted one corner of Morpheus' lips. "Oh, no. I am very much in charge tonight. It seems lazy to make you entirely responsible for coming up with our… *interludes*."

"*Fuck*," Hugh said, a little pulse of precome drooling from the tip of his cock before it succumbed to gravity and dripped onto whatever served as the platform beneath the stocks.

"Yes, I daresay that much is a foregone conclusion," Morpheus agreed. "Now, my pretty little captive human—do tell me. Will you be able to stay still and compliant while my guests and I amuse ourselves with you this evening? It wouldn't do for me to provide them with entertainment that squirms and begs for mercy all night. That would be *highly* distracting, given the important work we have to do."

A new hand appeared from behind him, out of his line of sight. Smooth fingertips trailed along the small of his back and over his left buttock before giving it an assessing squeeze. Hugh yelped and jerked, his cock jumping.

"That does not bode terribly well, does it?" said the Morpheus behind him. Hugh hadn't even heard him approach.

"N-no," he stammered. "I don't think I can stay still."

"Thank you for your honesty, my dearest plaything," the original Morpheus told him. "In that case, I will assist you. Drink this, please."

A small goblet appeared in his field of view. Morpheus raised it to Hugh's lips, supporting his chin as he tipped the contents slowly into Hugh's mouth. The liquid that rolled over his tongue was thick and faintly briny, but balanced with a hint of unexpected sweetness. He swallowed convulsively, aware that he had tasted something like it before, but unable to remember the context.

Almost immediately, languid warmth spread outward from his throat and stomach, dragging the shivery tension from his muscles in its wake. He moaned as Morpheus pulled the cup away, unable to stop the expression of tremulous relief as his body went limp and heavy. The carefully padded contraption he was shackled to supported him, keeping him upright and splayed open even as his legs turned to jelly. Only his cock remained at attention, twitching restlessly… the occasional dribble of seed stretching down from the tip.

"Much better," Morpheus said approvingly, stroking gentle fingers over Hugh's cheek. He hummed and tried to press into the contact, but even that much suddenly felt like an awful lot of work.

"Shall I open him up for our use?" offered the Morpheus standing behind him. The fingers on Hugh's arse cheek trailed lower, sliding over his entrance. Hugh's cock jumped so hard that it bounced against his stomach, leaving behind a sticky smear in the trail of coarse hair running down from his navel.

"If you would be so kind," said the first Morpheus, who tangled a hand in Hugh's hair and used the grip to raise his limp head. "It will save time later."

Floating and hazy with pleasure, Hugh watched the Morpheus in front of him unbutton the fall of his trousers and feed his erect cock into Hugh's slack mouth. A moment later, something slick dribbled between his arse cheeks. The fingers that had been teasing his hole pressed inside, finding almost no resistance.

Hugh hung lax in his bondage, sparks zipping along his nerves as a thick cock fucked his face and long fingers scissored open his hole, rubbing across his prostate carelessly. Time was meaningless as his body rocked between the twin sensations, heat coiling deeper and tighter in his balls with each stroke.

The dick thrusting into his throat gradually sped up its rhythm, its owner making a low noise of appreciation above him. He was pretty sure there were four fingers in his arse by the time his hot mouthful swelled impossibly further and throbbed—the only warning he got before thick ropes of spend spurted down his throat.

Hugh's balls drew up, ready to follow even though no one had so much as touched his dick… but at the last moment, the fingers and the softening cock in his mouth withdrew in unison. He hung there, trapped on the edge, unable to thrash or cry out in frustration as the sensation slowly subsided to a dull, throbbing ache between his legs.

"Perfect." The Morpheus in front of him tucked himself neatly away in his trousers, sounding completely unaffected by his climax. "Here, let me finish readying him for the evening, and we can get back to the important matters we have to discuss."

Inside, Hugh trembled with frustrated need. His body stayed slack and useless, however, as Morpheus tied a blindfold over his eyes and slipped earplugs into his ears. The sound of casual conversation dulled to a meaningless hum as the foam plugs swelled inside his ear canals, cutting off the outside world. The slow, steady thud of his heartbeat echoed in its place.

Morpheus' hand trailed down the length of his body as he moved to join his doppelganger behind Hugh. He wanted desperately to yelp as that hand grasped his cock and balls, tugging them down taut. A tight, constrictive band closed around the base. Some kind of rubber cock ring?

He managed the barest hint of a whimper as Morpheus fisted his trapped cock firmly, giving a slight twist of the wrist with every stroke until Hugh's balls strained to pull up tight and release their load. The cock ring was all that stood between him and an explosive, crashing orgasm.

Then, as unexpectedly as he'd begun, Morpheus released his grip, leaving Hugh once more on the cusp. Blind and deaf, he had no way of knowing if either of the Morpheuses was still nearby. But the seconds ticked onward, stretching into minutes with no further touches… no vibration of footsteps or movement of air against his bare skin.

He waited desperately for the terrible, unrealized tension of the spoiled orgasm to unravel. It did not. Helpless and drugged, he hung balanced on the knife's edge of climax, waiting for someone—*anyone*—to come back and use his body hard enough and long enough for that unbearable tension to finally snap.

FOURTEEN

HUGH FLOATED IN a state that could very accurately be described as dreamlike. He was aware, on some level, that most people would find his current situation humiliating, if not downright disturbing.

But those hypothetical other people probably hadn't been tasked with preventing the end of the world, and therefore they probably weren't quite as desperate for a reprieve from the unrelenting pressure of external events as he was. If you put aside the casual dehumanization of it all, being sprawled in a dream-contraption that could never make you sore or cut off your circulation, while numerous exact copies of your lover randomly appeared to stick their dicks in you or jerk off and ejaculate randomly on your face, wasn't a half bad gig.

The elixir that had sapped the strength from his muscles was slowly weakening over time. Even so, Hugh had stopped whimpering and jerking weakly whenever a cock nudged at his arse or his lips and firmly thrust inside, partly because of how often it happened, but mostly because of how good it felt. Morpheus—the real one—hadn't been lying about taking the reins of this dream. Every thrust from behind plowed Hugh's prostate. The come on his face never dried or grew cold and sticky.

Most importantly, with the pounding his prostate was taking, he should have climaxed multiple times by now, even with the rubber cock ring. But apparently, Morpheus controlled that, too. Instead, Hugh had spent so long stranded on an impossibly lofty pre-orgasmic plateau that everything was beginning to run together into a single smear of ecstasy, shot through with shiny threads of desperate need.

It might have been hours, or it might have simply been the function of the strange, taffy-like consistency of time in the dream world. Deaf and blind as he was, Hugh couldn't even start to guess how many Morpheus-copies had taken their pleasure from him, how many times or in how many ways.

When fingers breached his oversensitive hole instead of a cock, and a fist encircled his aching erection in a firm, unyielding grip, he started sobbing unashamedly with relief. The climax that gathered at the base of his spine, ricocheting up to tingle along his scalp and down to curl his toes, was simply too big for his body to contain any other way.

The sobs grew into a scream, an eternity of being held on the edge erupting in what felt like *gallons* of spunk shooting out of his cock and balls to puddle on the platform beneath him. The fingers inside him curled into a fist, stretching him in ways he'd never been stretched before. That sent a fresh round of jerking spasms through his insides, until passing out seemed like a completely rational response to the signals his nerves were sending out.

Could you pass out inside a dream?

Certainly, his awareness went even hazier than before, and he couldn't have said how he transitioned from hanging blindfolded from sex furniture to lying peacefully in the embrace of a lithe body, stretched out on a comfortable mattress.

"I believe it's called 'waking up,' my hunter," said an amused voice.

"Mmph," Hugh managed, not entirely sure he'd ever walk again. His body was doing an interesting buzzy, floaty thing, and trying to process words was distracting from it unnecessarily. He burrowed a bit further into Morpheus, hoping to get the point across.

"Yes, yes," Morpheus said, still with that amused lilt. "I trust you are sufficiently clear now, regarding your place in my arms, and not another's?"

Hugh contemplated that for a few moments. "Dunno," he slurred against the crook of Morpheus' shoulder. "Might need… 'nother reminder soon."

"I shall take it under consideration." Affection laced the velvet voice. "Rest now. I will stay with you until you return to sleep. Then I fear I must depart for a time."

Hugh chose to engage with the first part of that pronouncement, and ignore the second. Moments later, he was out like a snuffed candle.

Waking up the second time was disorientating—not least because he was pretty sure his body should be aching in some rather unique ways, and it wasn't.

"Gods," he moaned. "*Why* did I think entering a sexual relationship with a supernatural being was a good idea, again?"

The answer, of course, was because it was Morpheus. And because the sex was actually mind-blowing if you could get past the disturbing psychological implications of some of it. In the absence of the physical effects he should have been experiencing, he felt amazingly light and shockingly well-rested.

Mind you, he'd also gone to bed shortly after six p.m., and while he had no idea of the current hour, it was at least daytime outside. Hugh decided to accept what he'd been given. And given, and given, and *given*. After the whole 'bacchanal, drunk in a field, possessed by a god' thing, he'd probably needed the recovery time.

Somewhat unexpectedly, Morpheus must have, er, cleaned him up after he'd presumably shot his entire load into his pajama pants. *Again*.

Eight hundred was a bit old for wet dreams by any standard. However, when you were dating the actual God of Dreams—who also happened to be a surprisingly creative pervert—Hugh supposed it counted as extenuating circumstances.

He got up, still surprised when all his limbs worked more or less the way they were supposed to, and found Baphometh pacing outside his closed bedroom door.

"*Meow!*" said the cat, with uncharacteristic urgency.

Hugh felt a slight pang of guilt at the reminder that the animal had been feeling poorly the day before.

"Sorry, Baph," he apologized. "Want to try some cat food again? I'm afraid I'm out of sardines."

He threw on a ratty robe and led the way to the back room, disappointed to find the bowl of yesterday's kibble still sitting untouched. Baph gave it a disgusted look, stalking restlessly back and forth near the room's interior door with what seemed to be real distress.

Christ. Hugh really *was* going to end up trying to take a feral cat to the nearest veterinarian during an unfolding global apocalypse, wasn't he?

"No offense, furball," he said. "But your timing is *truly* awful."

He turned to pick up the food bowl, wondering if soaking the kibbles in water or broth might make them easier to eat. When he turned back, a naked man with dark chest hair, a scarred face, and part of one ear missing was standing on the far side of the room.

Hugh shrieked and dropped the bowl, hundreds of kibbles scattering across the floor with a chaotic skittering noise.

"Mate," said the naked stranger, "I am so sick of eating dried cat food I could *puke*. Can't we order in some sushi or somethin'?"

FIFTEEN

"WHAT?" HUGH SAID, a bit desperately. "I mean, seriously… *what is even happening right now*?"

The naked stranger shrugged. "Dunno. Sushi, I hope?" He took a couple of overly cautious steps, picking his legs up comically high. "Whoa. This is seriously *mental*. It's, like, when you're trying to catch a butterfly, but it's flying too high, so you have to bumble around on your hind legs like a complete twat and catch it with your front paws."

He paused, staring at his hands. His heavy brows furrowed as he opened and closed them. "These are pretty mint, though. *Love* the thumbs. Dead useful, innit?"

Hugh blinked. The naked stranger didn't disappear, so he tried it again with the same result. Then, something occurred to him. "Hang on. Is this another dream? That's it, isn't it? I didn't really wake up. I only *thought* I woke up, and this is some kind of… dream within a dream. Dream-ception."

The strange man in Hugh's boot room tilted his head, contemplating that.

"Nah," he said after a moment. "Pretty sure if it was a dream, my stomach wouldn't feel like my throat's been cut."

Convinced he'd figured out the answer, Hugh nodded sagely. "Whatever you say, friend. Tell you what. I'll just drive into Leatherhead and pick you up some sushi. I needed to go shopping anyway, yeah? And no one actually delivers out here. It's too rural."

With a put-upon sigh, the man casually licked his wrist and rubbed his arm over his tousled hair a couple of times, slicking it into place.

He fixed Hugh with a beady glare. "Fine. Don't take too long, though."

"I'll hurry," Hugh assured him, and fled the room. Scattered kitty kibble crunched underfoot as he left.

⎯⎯⎯◆⎯⎯⎯

Ninety minutes later, Hugh sat in his kitchen, watching a dream-hallucination delicately work its way through a value-pack of supermarket sushi. He was pointedly ignoring the exceptionally non-dreamlike nature of his grocery run—which had included snarled traffic, random strangers cursing at him for being in their way, and Hugh's preferred brand of crisps being out of stock.

He had at least managed to bribe his unwanted guest into putting on a T-shirt and a pair of track pants—both of which hung loose on his scrawny frame. Hugh watched as the last piece of tuna nori disappeared. The man licked bits of sticky rice neatly from his fingers, and sighed in satisfaction.

"Brills," he said, before wandering out of the kitchen.

Hugh followed him, helpless to do otherwise, and stood in the doorway of the living room as he marched over to the window and flopped down on the floor in a weak sunbeam. A moment later, soft snores emanated from the relaxed figure.

"What," Hugh said again, since he still felt that no one had satisfactorily answered that question. He gave himself a sharp pinch on the arm. His surroundings remained unchanged.

Or, rather, they remained *mostly* unchanged. Hugh swallowed another undignified yelp as a dark figure stepped out of nowhere with an owl perched on its shoulder.

"Hugh," Morpheus said, with uncharacteristic urgency. "There is news. I have received word from—"

He cut himself off, his blue gaze falling on the snoring intruder asleep on Hugh's floor.

"Um… yeah," Hugh said, rubbing a palm over the back of his skull. "*About* that…"

Iridaceae flapped down from Morpheus' shoulder in an excited flutter of wings. She transformed as she hit the ground, bouncing over to the stranger like an excited child.

"Baph!" she exclaimed, shaking the figure's arm. "You're human!"

The man peeled open a bleary eye, a hiss of irritation escaping his lips. Then he seemed to register who was kneeling over him. His eyes grew wide, and he rolled into a sitting position.

"Ir!" He held out his arms as though showing them off. "Yeah! Isn't it aces? I got hungry, and all this arsehole would give me was that boring dry cat food. So, I changed like you do, and I got him to bring me sushi!"

Hugh found himself staring at the pair with his jaw hanging open. It was still hanging open when he turned back to Morpheus, desperate for the God of

Dreams to laugh at him and say some version of, "Gotcha! Bet you thought all this was *real*, didn't you?"

Instead, he found his lover frowning at the scene with a distinct expression of disquiet. As though sensing Hugh's regard, Morpheus turned and took him by the arm, leading him out of the room.

As soon as they were away from the happy pair comparing opposable thumbs in the living room, Morpheus whirled to face Hugh.

"We appear to have a problem," he said grimly.

Hugh couldn't hold back a shrill bark of laughter. He was aware of the hysterical edge behind it. "You *think*? This is a dream, though, isn't it? Cats don't just wake up one morning and randomly change into humans!" He shook his head sharply. "Not in the *real* world, I mean."

Morpheus took a careful breath, his chest rising and falling. He still held Hugh's arm in a firm grip… which was probably just as well, since Hugh was starting to feel decidedly lightheaded.

"I have told you many times, my hunter. The Sublunary is no more and no less real than the Night Lands, or any other realm." He glanced over Hugh's shoulder, looking in the direction from which they'd come. "I fear you are very much awake right now, and this is very much real."

Hugh shook his head slowly back and forth in confusion. "So… you're telling me that my stray cat is some kind of shape-shifter? Like Iridaceae?"

Morpheus hesitated. "Perhaps it would be best to start from the beginning. Come."

He led Hugh back to the kitchen, where the remains of a jumbo sushi tray lay haphazardly on the table. Hugh sank down into a chair, and Morpheus pulled up a second one to sit next to him.

"I told you there was news," he began. "In fact, Dionysus was good to his word. He has spoken with the Titans in the Pit."

Hugh latched onto this pronouncement, which in his current level of insanity seemed somehow easier to deal with than the scene they'd just left behind in the living room. "Oh, yes? What did they tell him?"

The concern in Morpheus' expression was not, to put it mildly, all that reassuring.

"The Titans foretell of the coming of a new God of Hope," he said simply.

Hugh took that in for a moment.

"All right. But… that's *good*, isn't it?" he asked. "I mean, if all our current problems are because the old Goddess of Hope is gone… then getting a new one seems like a step in the right direction. Doesn't it?"

Morpheus continued to watch Hugh with that same worried expression.

"Perhaps," he said. "However, I came to a rather startling revelation in the wake of my cousin's report. You and I traveled across the mortal world, and yet the remnants of hope in the Sublunary did not enter my sister's repaired *pithos*."

Feeling like he was running about two steps behind his companion, Hugh frowned. "Well, no. But it could just mean that we repaired the *pithos* wrong.

Or that there's some magical incantation we don't know about, or maybe—"

"The remnants of hope in the Sublunary did not enter Elpis' vessel... because they were entering *you*," Morpheus said, cutting him off. "Hugh—you are becoming a god."

Hugh stared at him blankly. "Could you repeat that? Because for a second there, it sounded like you just said I was becoming a—"

"A god," Morpheus said again. "Look around. Observe what is happening. You have taken a familiar. You are gathering my sister's power inside yourself. You are becoming the embodiment of Hope in the world."

Hugh continued to stare.

The silence lengthened.

"Well, *that's* a load of old bollocks if I ever heard one," he finally said.

From the living room, the sound of happy laughter rang out as an owl and a pussycat reintroduced themselves in a brand-new way.

SIXTEEN

MORPHEUS HAD FEARED that the news of Hugh's incipient godhood might cause some sort of acute psychological damage—one of many new fears which had beset him since speaking with Dionysus. Instead, Hugh appeared intent on rejecting the claim outright.

This was, perhaps, understandable given the circumstances. Unfortunately, they did not have the time for it. The moment Phantasos or, fates forbid, *Phobetor* learned of this new development, Hugh would become a target for immediate destruction. It had been bad enough when the human had drawn their attention as potential bait or ransom for Morpheus—now he would become Phobetor's enemy in his own right.

Perhaps, if their theories about Elpis' death and the growing imbalance in the mortal realm were correct, he would become Phobetor's *greatest* enemy.

And Hugh was still dangerously weak.

After speaking to Dionysus, Morpheus had harbored hopes that his hypothesis was incorrect. But now, Hugh's animal familiar sat in the other room with a freshly constructed human body, and that faint hope had been dashed.

He reached across the small space separating them and took Hugh's hands in his. Hugh glanced up at him, startled—their gazes locking and holding.

"I am sorry, my hunter," Morpheus told him. "I cannot express how much. But there is no mistake."

Hugh's head shook slowly back and forth in negation. "No, but… I can't be a god. I'm just, y'know… just *me!*"

Morpheus squeezed the callused hands cradled in his. "Do you recall what you told me in 1321 AD? I came upon you looting a baron's granary to feed your village during a famine, with no certainty that the crops would not fail again the following year. You looked me in the eye and told me, 'It takes a lot of hope to make it through a century'."

A look of pained desperation crept into Hugh's expression.

"Well, *yes*, but that doesn't mean…" He trailed off, his tone growing uncertain.

"You are eight hundred years old," Morpheus continued inexorably. "The oldest human who has ever lived. You have seen some of the worst humanity has to offer — and, I dearly hope, some of the best. Through all of it, you still choose to stay with them, year after year. Who else in all the realms is better suited to take up my sister's mantle?"

If anything, the look of fear on Hugh's face grew deeper. "But… is it even possible for something like that to happen? A human becoming a god? Is that even, like, a *thing*?"

The question pierced directly into the heart of Morpheus' own misgivings. Such an event was completely unprecedented. There was no guarantee that a body which had once been mortal could contain the amount of raw power inherent in full godhood. The possibility existed that Hugh would only be able to encompass a certain amount of hope before his corporeal form simply disintegrated under the strain.

The mere act of thinking about it brought a terrifying tightness to Morpheus' chest—worse, even, than the debilitating weakness and illness he'd experienced as a mortal after Phobetor had stolen his opal pendant.

"I think we must work on the assumption that it is, indeed, possible," he managed. "I wish you to travel to the Night Lands with me. We must make plans, and I would prefer to do so there rather than here."

"In my dreams, you mean?" Hugh asked, still looking dazed and wrongfooted by events. "I just woke up a few hours ago."

"No, not in dreams," Morpheus replied. "I wish you to accompany me in your corporeal form. Consider it an experiment, if you will."

Hugh frowned, his heavy eyebrows drawing together like storm clouds. "So... what, then? Do you need to possess me? Dionysus said it was easy to drag me to the Night Lands when he was in my body. Does that mean you can possess people, too?"

"In fact, Dionysus specified that your physical form was *surprisingly* easy to transport," Morpheus corrected. "That clarification is telling. However, to answer your question—I assume that I could possess a human, should the need ever arise. I have simply never chosen to do so... and I do not believe it will be necessary now."

Hugh slid his hands free from Morpheus' light grip, looking decidedly unconvinced. "I'm not sure what you're basing that on."

"Supposition," Morpheus said, rising from his chair. "Come. Let us retrieve the others and depart."

Hugh stared up at him for a long moment before getting to his feet. "As long as you realize that I have no bloody clue how to travel between realms."

"With luck," Morpheus said, "we will remedy that oversight momentarily."

Hugh led the way back to the living room, shaking his head and muttering under his breath the whole time. In their absence, Iridaceae had moved to sit cross-legged on the sofa, while Baphometh curled on the floor next to her, looking up at her adoringly.

Morpheus suppressed a sigh. While he could not fault Hugh's choice of familiar, he had a feeling that Iridaceae was going to become even more insufferable than usual in the coming days.

The pair looked up as they entered.

Baphometh blinked amber-green eyes at Hugh. "Oi, mate. Better be careful with that scowl. You wouldn't want your face to freeze like that, would you?"

"I cannot believe I'm taking backtalk from my cat. In *English*, no less," Hugh said.

"We are returning to the Night Lands to regroup," Morpheus told them. "Hugh is becoming the new God of Hope."

Iridaceae peered at Hugh with a skeptical expression. "Is he really?"

Baphometh rose to his feet, stretching luxuriously. "*I* could have told you that, luv."

"Please attend us," Morpheus said. "There is much to discuss."

Iridaceae made a disgruntled noise, but she transformed and flew over to land on his shoulder. Baphometh rolled his eyes, but then a fluffy, black-haired cat sat where a human form had been a moment before. Hugh inhaled sharply, his right hand jerking up toward his chest.

"Ah," Morpheus said. "You felt it, then. He is utilizing your power to transform. In the normal course of things, it would be a negligible effort. You are still weak, however. And that is one of the first things we must address."

Hugh looked at him helplessly, one hand still resting over his heart as the cat freed himself from the oversized clothing he'd been wearing and trotted over, winding around his master's ankles.

"Morpheus... I don't think I can do this," he said carefully.

Morpheus steeled himself not to go to his lover. Not here. Not yet. "I am not entirely certain you have a choice, my hunter. I can only promise that you will not have to face this alone." He held out a hand. After a moment of painful hesitation, Hugh took it. "Follow me. We are going to a place you have visited many times. You remember Agnes' meadow? The oak tree?"

Hugh caught his breath. The idyllic setting was where his mind took him in dreams when times were hardest. Morpheus had, on occasion, shunted Hugh's sleeping mind there himself. It had been woven into the human's soul since he was mortal—a medieval blacksmith with his beloved, heavily pregnant wife. The scene had become imprinted within the realm of dreams over the course of centuries, and

Morpheus had ensured it remained there, ready and waiting whenever it was needed.

"Picture it well," he told Hugh. "For that is where we are going."

Unsure of what, exactly, would happen next, Morpheus focused on their destination and stepped through the veil with Iridaceae, pulling Hugh along behind him. His feet landed in soft grass. When he looked back, Hugh stood next to him, looking around at their surroundings with something like awe. The black cat was there as well, still rubbing against his legs.

"How...?" Hugh breathed, staring up at the towering branches of the oak tree, clad in the pale green finery of early spring.

A strange tangle of pride and trepidation twisted in Morpheus' chest. While it was true that there had been little question before, now, there was none at all.

"It will take you time to master the skill. But as you gain more power, distance will become as nothing to you," he said gently. "Let us make ourselves comfortable. We have many things to consider."

Hugh dragged his eyes away from the idealized vision of a thirteenth-century meadow. He was still gaping openly as he met Morpheus' gaze, but wonder had begun to creep into his expression, edging out the fear.

SEVENTEEN

"I DON'T EVEN understand what being the god of something *entails*," Hugh said. The tree bark at his back was rough and familiar; the scent of grass and other growing things a soothing reminder of simpler times. His hand trailed idly through soft black hair, the rhythmic motion going some way toward calming the fluttery panic rising in his chest.

They'd fetched up in a position Hugh remembered through the blurry lens of dreams. He sat with his legs stretched out before him, leaning against the bole of a massive oak that only survived in memory. Morpheus lay prone, his head resting in Hugh's lap. His eyes were closed, brows furrowed in thought.

Moments after they'd arrived, Iridaceae had transformed only long enough to say, "Come on, Baph! You *have* to see this forest!" Then the unlikely pair were off in a scramble of wings and paws, disappearing from view.

For his own mental health, Hugh had decided to put aside the whole *'cat turning into a human'* thing, at least for now. He knew, intellectually, that such transformations were possible. Iridaceae was proof of that much. It was the idea that he was somehow responsible for Baphometh becoming a scruffy bloke with a taste for tuna nigiri that he couldn't quite cope with at the moment.

Not on top of everything else.

"I would say," Morpheus began, with the air of someone who had given the subject considerable thought, "that as gods, we are the nexus of a series of systems. As you have seen, the temporary absence of a god does not result in the instant extinction of that god's domain. Hope still exists without my sister. Living creatures still dreamed during my imprisonment on Earth."

Hugh's hand stilled. "But in your absence — and your sister's — hopes and dreams began to twist and weaken in the mortal realm."

"Correct." Morpheus blinked startling blue eyes open, gazing up at him. "Even here in the Night Lands, the systems begin to wind down over time. And my sister has been gone for millennia. I believe our first order of business will be to determine what, if anything, remains of Elpis' realm."

Hugh filed the notion that he was expected to have a *realm* next to the growing collection of other things that his brain wasn't currently equipped to handle. "And our second order of business?"

"We must expose you to more hope. As much as we possibly can." Morpheus rolled into a sitting position, facing him. "We must make you stronger, before either of my brothers discover what has happened."

Hugh made a valiant effort to consider logistics. Their previous travels, when they'd still been trying to refill the *pithos*, had been dangerous and time-consuming given the state of the world under Phobetor's growing influence. They had also made a significant dent in Hugh's not inconsiderable savings.

"Look," he said. "I'm not poor by any means, but I stopped bothering with extreme wealth accumulation some time ago. I can finance a few more trips, but with inflation out of control and so much of the world's infrastructure crumbling—"

Morpheus reached forward, placing a hand over one of Hugh's. His jaw snapped shut.

"You misunderstand, my hunter," said the God of Dreams. "We are not bound by human modes of travel. Once you gain a modicum of proficiency with moving through the veil, you will be able to direct us to places where hope still abounds, as easily as stepping from one room to the next."

The temptation to toss this latest declaration straight onto the *'do not think about'* pile was nearly overwhelming. Hugh resisted it with difficulty.

"I don't know how to do that, Morpheus," he said carefully.

The hand covering his gave him a reassuring squeeze. "You underestimate yourself. How did you follow me here?"

Hugh blinked. "You were holding my hand. You pulled me along behind you."

"Not strictly true," Morpheus said. "Had I taken the hand of any normal human and stepped through the veil, from their perspective, it would have seemed that my hand melted into nothing and I disappeared."

Hugh's breath caught in response to this new piece of evidence. He didn't like the way things seemed to be piling up in support of this not being some kind of massive misunderstanding. "But—"

Morpheus shook his head. "I asked you to picture this place as we stepped through the veil. So… again. Tell me how you followed me here."

Hugh's throat worked against a dry swallow. "I did what you said. I pictured it in my mind. Then you tugged on my hand, and when I took a step forward, it felt like I was pushing aside an invisible curtain or something."

"That was the veil." Morpheus slid his hand away. Hugh missed it immediately. "Not only did you travel through it, but you ensured that your familiar accompanied you. To follow the pull of hope through the veil will not take much more effort."

That... wasn't as reassuring a prospect as Morpheus probably intended it to be. Hugh firmly put aside visions of being randomly tugged to new locations scattered across the world like something out of *Quantum Leap* or *Sliders*.

"You said that was the *second* order of business," he said.

"Indeed." Morpheus rose gracefully to his feet and reached a hand down. Hugh took it, allowing himself to be pulled upright by that unexpected, wiry strength. "I doubt that anything remains of Elpis' original realm, given that all memory of her has been erased. However, we should try to find you someplace within my domain that calls to you. Perhaps..." And here, his expression turned sour for an instant before he consciously smoothed it. "Something abutting Dionysus' realm might be appropriate. That way you would be flanked by allies on both sides."

He indicated a direction with the sweep of one long-fingered hand. Hugh turned that way, wondering how, exactly, a piece of imaginary land was supposed to call to him. Feeling foolish, he stretched his senses outward, trying to imagine what might lie beyond this current vision of a medieval clearing.

An instant later, he felt an insistent mental tug in almost the exact opposite direction from where Morpheus was pointing. He turned toward the sensation, startled.

"Erm..." he said.

Morpheus frowned. "Phantasos' realm lies in that direction. I do not think—"

But it was too late. Hugh started walking without making any kind of a conscious decision to do so. It was as though he was lost in the desert, desperate with thirst, and a cool drink awaited him somewhere ahead.

Morpheus kept pace with him, looking increasingly alarmed as the meadow around them smeared into undifferentiated watercolors. "Hugh, I cannot protect you outside of my own realm. If my brother—"

The sense of moving through great distances in the blink of an eye increased until their surroundings became little more than a gray blur. Hugh didn't feel as though he was hurrying, exactly. More like his steps had become gigantic, covering miles with each stride. The pull of comfort and familiarity drew him onward, until eventually, he reached the source.

He stumbled to a stop. Morpheus, still beside him, grasped him by the elbow to steady him. Hugh leaned over, bracing his hands on his knees and dragging in great, gasping breaths. The air, if there even *was* proper air in the Night Lands, hit his lungs like the finest wine hit one's bloodstream. It was heady, intoxicating—yet also somehow nourishing. His head swam with it, even as fresh strength and vitality flooded his muscles.

"Wh-what happened?" he choked out, still bent over. "Where *are* we?"

Morpheus continued to support him with a one-handed grip as he looked around in evident surprise. "I... am not entirely certain."

Hugh pushed upright, his swimming head protesting the movement for only a moment before his surroundings began to register properly. They were standing on a rocky slope, desolation extending around them in all directions.

Or rather... in all directions but *one*.

Hugh stared at the bubbling spring emanating from a crack in the ancient stone. It wasn't large, but it wasn't exactly small, either. And around the burbling water, life had sprung up. Clinging to the crumbling shale, a profusion of flowers and leaves dripped down the side of the rocky hill. Butterflies flitted lazily from bloom to bloom, and hummingbirds jousted with each other in hopes of claiming the richest sources of nectar.

As Hugh watched, the little oasis appeared to reach toward him, tender shoots and vines unfurling before his eyes. He ripped his gaze away, turning toward the only other source of beauty in this strange and contradictory place. Morpheus turned at the same moment, their eyes locking in mutual understanding.

"It's here," Hugh said hoarsely. "This is the place. Morpheus... this is what's left of your sister's realm."

EIGHTEEN

MORPHEUS STARED AT their unfamiliar surroundings in consternation. He had existed within the Night Lands, in one form or another, for countless eons. There should be no part of it that was completely unknown to him.

And yet, he could not have said how he and Hugh came to be in this tiny oasis among the rocks. He could not have pointed in a given direction and stated, *'here is the border with my realm; Phantasos' realm lies over there.'*

"How is this possible?" he said, reaching down to touch a flowering vine that rippled toward Hugh's feet.

His companion was still breathing heavily, panic and yearning fighting for dominance in his expression. Hugh reached for Morpheus, and his lover's grip on his forearm trembled with some unnamed, overwhelming emotion.

"Morpheus," Hugh's voice was a raspy whisper. "I'm *so thirsty.*"

Instinct urged Morpheus to be cautious. Nonetheless, he could see no conceivable way this could be a trap for them. Hugh had begun to manifest his nascent godhood before Morpheus had even arrived to warn him about Dionysus' news. Hugh had been the one to bring them here, as though compelled.

And now, Hugh thirsted. They were standing next to an impossible wellspring, set in an impossible place that should not exist. And he *thirsted.*

"Hope springs eternal," Morpheus murmured. Taking a deep breath, he turned to Hugh. "I believe we should drink. Only, allow me to drink first, in case I am wrong and this is some sort of ruse."

For the briefest of instants, Hugh swelled up with protective anger, as though he might shove Morpheus down the mountainside rather than let him near the spring. Then he gasped, jerking his hand away from Morpheus' arm as though it had burned him and taking a hasty step backwards.

"I don't..." he began. "I... don't know what just came over me. It's like I need to protect the water, even though I know you don't mean this place any harm. Morpheus, what's *happening* to me?"

It was true. This could be no ruse.

"You are becoming a god, my hunter." Morpheus stepped back, ceding the space to his sister's chosen successor. "The spring is yours. Drink deep. I suspect the water needs you as much as you need the water."

Hugh stared at him for several more seconds, his chest rising and falling rapidly. Then, he broke—lunging for the bubbling rivulet and falling to his knees next to it. He cupped his hands under the tiny flow, where it emerged from a crack in the stone, bringing the water to his lips over and over.

Realizing the obvious, Morpheus reached into his robes and pulled out his sister's infuriating *pithos*. He had cursed the item relentlessly over the past days, berating it for not collecting hope as he had assumed it would.

Now, he moved slowly to join Hugh, careful not to startle him, and held the mouth of the clay jar beneath the wellspring. Clear water trickled merrily into the vessel. When it was full, Morpheus handed it to Hugh, who looked up at him from his knees as though Morpheus had hung the moon and stars.

Hugh drank like he had been lost in the wilderness for days. Water ran down his chin, dripping onto his shirt.

"More," he gasped, when the *pithos* was empty.

Morpheus helped him steady it beneath the flow, hovering nearby as Hugh drained it a second time, and then a third. All the while, new growth spread around them like an ever-expanding green carpet. The smell of flowers and tender new leaves hung in the air.

Hugh set the clay jar down among the creeping plants, finally sated. He looked up at Morpheus, his eyes glowing molten bronze.

"It's going to be all right now," he said, a strange resonance behind his voice. "I don't know how I know that, but I really think things are going to be okay."

Morpheus knew, with a terrible certainty, that their path would not be so straightforward. Nevertheless, he sank to his knees in front of the man who had accepted him and cherished him despite the vast gulf separating them, and kissed him.

Hugh leaned into him like one of the flowers around them seeking the sun, only to pull back, startled, when an owl and a cat arrived at the edge of the little oasis in a flurry of feathers and fur.

The two familiars transformed, both of them appearing suspiciously disheveled. Iridaceae, in particular, looked flustered. A mark strongly resembling a love bite emerged, half hidden, from the collar of her simple shirt.

"What's going on?" she demanded, peering suspiciously around at the burgeoning plant life. "This place feels strange!"

"Finally found his realm, it looks like," Baphometh said. "Bit of a pain in the arse having it halfway up a mountain, though."

Hugh blinked, and the liquid metal gleam of his eyes faded back to earthy brown. "How did you find us? And… wait. Have you two been—"

"Big old explosion of energy, wasn't there?" Baphometh looked around with interest.

"It *was* kind of difficult to miss," Iridaceae agreed, frowning.

Morpheus caught his breath, as the implication of that set in. "This realm is undefended," he realized. "It was hidden before. But if these two sensed it coming out of hiding, that means—"

A broad figure swirled into existence, an ivy-wrapped staff clasped in his hand and a fresh wine stain still damp on his loose white tunic, as though he had spilled his drink in surprise.

"Cousin," Dionysus said. "What in the gods' realms are *you* doing up here?"

"There have been… developments," Morpheus said, in a serious disservice to understatement. "Evidently, the Titans were correct in their prophecy. There is, indeed, a new God of Hope in the offing. And now, I urgently require your assistance."

Dionysus frowned, his attention falling first on the two familiars, and then on Hugh. His eyes widened in sudden understanding.

"Oh," he said. "Your human is becoming a god? Fates, is that even possible?"

"That's what *I* said!" Hugh told him, a bit plaintively.

"Possible or not, it is happening before our eyes," Morpheus snapped. "This was the last remnant of Elpis' domain. With the return of its ruler, it is *growing*. We must erect defenses to conceal it before anyone else comes here and discovers what has occurred."

Dionysus appeared to be taking in the implications of this new revelation. "All right; all right. Don't get your robes in a twist, cousin. Hugh, do you know how to use your powers yet? Can you get some barriers around this place? Love the new temple, by the way."

"The new…" Hugh trailed off. He turned back, following Dionysus' gaze to where a familiar, homey cottage appeared to be assembling itself in the side of the mountain, a short distance upslope of the wellspring. "What the *actual fuck*…?"

"We must focus," Morpheus said, bringing them back to the point. "Hugh does not yet have either the power or the knowledge to defend his realm, small though it is. We need to protect this area, before those who would wish him harm discover it."

A whirl of gold and white resolved into another familiar figure. Morpheus' stomach sank.

Phantasos scowled, the ugly expression sitting uncomfortably on his pretty features. "Before *who* discovers *what*?" he demanded, gazing around the growing meadow suspiciously.

NINETEEN

HUGH TORE HIS attention away from the perfect replica of his cottage on Earth that appeared to be burrowing itself into the side of the mountain. His gaze fell on an all-too-handsome, all-too-familiar face topped by artful waves of honey-blond hair. Before he could even draw breath, an upswelling of hot rage erupted inside his chest like a volcano at the idea of the fucking God of Fantasy even daring to *look* on this place.

"Oh, *hell* no," he said, taking two steps forward and landing a solid right hook to Phantasos' perfect cheekbone, before his higher brain functions could decide whether that was a wise idea or not.

The pretty god's face jerked an inch to the side beneath the force of the blow, and instantly, an answering expression of outrage twisted his sculpted features.

"How *dare* you lay hands on me, human worm?" he spat, placing one manicured hand in the center of Hugh's chest and shoving hard.

Hugh *knew* the power behind that shove. He knew that, by rights, he should have gone flying through the air, landing against sharp stone with enough force to shatter bones. Instead, he rooted his feet to the unmoving stone of this place that had called to his soul like a siren song, not giving an inch of ground. His lips pulled back, baring his teeth in an animal snarl.

Phantasos took a shocked step backward, propelled by some combination of surprise and the unspent force of his push.

"What...?" he sputtered. "What is the meaning of this trick?"

"It is no trick, brother." Morpheus stepped up to stand shoulder to shoulder with Hugh, and Hugh loved him just a little bit more for not trying to stand in front of him like some kind of protector.

A moment later, Dionysus stepped up on Hugh's other side, smelling of uninhibited sex and spilled wine. "Apparently, you're trespassing on someone else's property, lad."

"What are you *talking* about?" Phantasos cast his gaze around the area. "This is *my domain!*"

"Look again," Morpheus said coldly. "Tell me that you were even aware of the existence of this spring five minutes ago. It is no more your domain than it is mine, for all that it now borders both places."

Hugh had learned centuries ago that there were few things uglier than a handsome face twisted in hatred. That maxim held true now, as the perfect features that had launched a thousand desires collapsed into sullen lines.

"If it's not yours and it's not mine, then who's is it?" Phantasos hissed. His angry brown eyes snapped fire, moving to land on Dionysus. "Surely not *yours*, cousin. It doesn't reek of debauchery in the same way you do."

Dionysus sighed. "I'd hoped your brother was wrong when he said you'd turned your allegiance toward the darkness. Why is the God of Fantasy so filled with anger?"

"Why is the God of Wine not hiding away in his palace and *minding his own damned business*?" Phantasos shot back.

Hugh took an aggressive step forward. The others flanked him. "Because Phobetor is trying to destroy the world, you piss-guzzling little prick," he said. "Now go the fuck away, before I decide to test whether drinking this water means I can kick you in the balls and have it actually make an impression."

Phantasos took a wary half-step backward, scowling between the three men standing abreast, and the two familiars hanging back behind them. "*You* drank the water here? Why?"

"I expect he was thirsty," Dionysus said, a tone of disquiet creeping into his normally booming voice.

Too late, Hugh realized that he probably shouldn't have said that, if the goal was to keep it a secret that Elpis had christened him as her successor.

Phantasos looked from Hugh to Baphometh and back again, his brow furrowed. "You?" he murmured. "No, that makes no sense. You are *human*."

"My foot. Your testicles," Hugh threatened again, preparing to take a run-up.

Morpheus placed a quelling hand on his shoulder. "Leave now, brother. You are not welcome here. You are also, I hasten to add, *outnumbered*."

Phantasos stepped back again, letting out an incredulous bark of laughter. "Is that a *threat*, brother? Tell me, what weapons does the God of Dreams possess against another god? Phobetor has bested you at every turn!"

"The God of Dreams *and Nightmares*," Morpheus said. "Do not forget that."

Even before he turned to look, Hugh could feel the weight of inky shadows spilling from his lover's gaze and billowing toward Phantasos. Iridaceae, back in her owl form, hooted in threat and flew over to land on her master's shoulder. Somewhat to Hugh's shock, a large black cat stalked forward to sit next to his feet, lifting a front paw and ostentatiously stretching out curved claws, one by one.

"What weapons does the God of *Fantasy* possess, cousin?" Dionysus asked mildly. "You have no business here, and your only ally is too busy breaking his toys in the Sublunary to come and help you now."

Something occurred to Hugh at the mention of Phobetor. "Hang on. Should we let him go, or should we take him prisoner? If he gets away, he's going to run straight to his brother, isn't he?"

"An interesting point," Morpheus said, taking a step forward.

Phantasos squeaked, his bravado cracking. He backpedaled as Morpheus' nightmare darkness continued to roll toward him, and a second later, he was gone in a swirl of glittering light.

"Shit," Hugh cursed. "*Should* we have tried to capture him?"

Dionysus grunted. "Doubt we could've. Not without some fancy spell work, anyway."

Hugh thought of the rune-inscribed magical chains that had held first Morpheus, and later, him. He shuddered.

The darkness surrounding Morpheus pulled back, fading away to nothing.

"We are ill-equipped to fight this war," he said, disgust creeping into his normally level tone. "Fortunately, so is Phantasos. However, it is more vital than ever that we erect protections around this place. You are correct that he will report what he has seen to Phobetor, Hugh."

Hugh swallowed. "Once again, I have no idea how to do that. Am I supposed to know?"

"No reason why you should, mate," Dionysus said. "Fortunately, you've got access to not only an overprotective boyfriend, but also a bloke who managed to lock down his own domain for quite a few centuries without anyone getting in. Sit back and relax for a bit. We'll get you sorted."

——◆——

For lack of any better options, Hugh did as he was told. He sat with Iridaceae perched on his shoulder and Baphometh curled watchfully at his side, listening as Morpheus and Dionysus discussed esoteric magic and debated how to deal with the fact that this place was still expanding in size.

Evidently, they came to some kind of an agreement on strategy after a few minutes of debate.

"This will drain power from the wellspring," Morpheus warned. "It is unavoidable, since only the realm itself can power its own wards."

Hugh was more prepared this time for the storm of protectiveness that bubbled up inside him. He swallowed it down, willing his heartbeat to slow. "Will it hurt the spring permanently?" he asked, not sure what he'd do if the answer was yes.

"No, no," Dionysus assured. "This place was basically nothing when you first arrived, and look at it now." He gestured at the lush greenery aggressively taking over the mountainside. "We'll craft the protections so they only take a percentage of the spring's energy, and grow as its power grows. It won't take long to recover from the initial strain."

Hugh looked to Morpheus for further reassurance, and received a nod.

He licked his lips. "Okay. Do it, then."

"I am giving myself access, if that is amenable to you," Morpheus said. "All others will require an express invitation to enter, assuming they can even find it."

Hugh frowned at Dionysus, who chuckled.

"Yes, even me. Though I'll still know where it is, at least. Phantasos will probably be able to find it as well, fair warning."

"So, he could lead Phobetor here?" Hugh asked, aware of the irony surrounding his fear of such a thing happening.

"Yes," Morpheus said. "However, they will be unable to enter without your permission."

"Better than nothing," Hugh told them.

"Indeed," Morpheus agreed.

Crafting wards, while impressive to think about, turned out to be surprisingly boring to watch. Baphometh curled his tail over his nose and started dozing, while Hugh turned inward, attempting to track the power drain as energy flowed outward from the water.

It was disconcerting to feel his own strength wane in concert with his surroundings, but the others had been telling the truth when they'd promised not to use too much. It was even more disconcerting when Hugh felt the finished wards snap into place. He gasped, feeling uncomfortably like a spider after someone had slammed a glass down on the countertop to trap it.

"There, done," Dionysus said unnecessarily.

"We can still leave, though, right?" Hugh asked, aware that they would need to go at some point, even if the very idea of being parted from this place filled him with misgivings.

"Oh, yes." Dionysus patted him on the shoulder that wasn't occupied with an owl, ignoring the glare Morpheus sent his way. "There are no barriers to exit, only to entry. And now, I think I should go and have a word with Thanatus, if I can track down the old bastard."

"Yes," Morpheus said grimly. "Perhaps you will have more success with him than I did. You may leave any messages for us at my palace. I have not locked it against outsiders. Not yet, at any rate."

"Very well," Dionysus replied. "I'd tell you both not to do anything I wouldn't do, but..."

"Quite," Morpheus said tartly.

Hugh rallied himself to stand, feeling the drain on the spring as though it was a drain on his own muscles. "Thanks, mate. For everything."

Dionysus made a considering noise. "Don't thank me. This is the most interesting thing to happen here since I went into seclusion." He ran a meaty hand down his face, stretching the skin. "Fuck, I need a drink first if I'm going to talk to that humorless arsehole."

"Down a bottle for me while you're at it," Hugh told him.

Dionysus made a vague gesture of agreement and swirled out of existence in a small maelstrom of ivy leaves. Alone with their familiars, Hugh and Morpheus locked gazes for a long moment. Exhaustion tugged at Hugh's limbs, but there was one more thing he needed to do.

"I want to look inside *that*," he said, pointing up the slope to the eerie replica of his cottage.

"Yes," Morpheus mused. "The appearance of this structure is curious. Dionysus called it a temple, but I'm not certain that explanation is the correct one."

Hugh led the way up the rocky path to the familiar front door. It was the new one, replaced after Phobetor's goons had broken in and destroyed the old one. The knob turned without resistance—unlocked.

He wasn't sure what he'd expected, but his familiar belongings strewn about exactly as they had been when Morpheus dragged him away to the Night Lands... wasn't it. Especially when the faint smell of fish going off greeted him in the kitchen, where a discarded sushi tray still sat on the table.

"Um…" Hugh said, looking around for any hint of this being a simulacrum.

"Intriguing," Morpheus said. "All is as you left it?"

"It… seems to be?" Hugh replied uncertainly.

In a daze, he continued deeper into the little house, all the way to the boot room and the back door. By any kind of sane logic, this door should be buried in the mountainside. Curious if he'd find sheer stone beyond, he grasped the knob and opened it, revealing…

He blinked rapidly, and looked again. "What? *How*?"

Morpheus joined him, gazing out at the gravel path leading past a stretch of green turf, with the forest beyond. The familiar view from his back door on Earth.

"That," Morpheus said slowly, "is somewhat unexpected."

TWENTY

INTRIGUED, MORPHEUS RETREATED to the front door again. This time, he felt the gossamer brush of the veil slide over him as he approached. "Hugh, come here," he called. "I believe I understand the mechanism behind what has happened."

That was, of course, a gross oversimplification. Iridaceae and Baphometh, who had been hanging back when he and Hugh had entered, passed over the threshold and joined them, still in animal form.

"Stop," Morpheus told Hugh, bringing him to a halt a step before the invisible barrier.

"What is it?" Hugh asked, wearing a dazed expression that Morpheus did not particularly like.

"Step forward, but remember the feeling of passing through the veil… as you did when you followed me to the Night Lands earlier," he said. "As far as I can determine, a gate in the barrier between the Night Lands and the Sublunary has now been made manifest in your front entryway."

"*What*?" Hugh asked again. But he did step forward, surprise sliding over his face as he passed through the ripple in reality. "Oh." He turned, looking toward the back of the cottage; then pivoted to face Morpheus and the two familiars. "Um… okay. But why is it doing that?"

Morpheus pressed his lips together, not fully pleased with the answer he was about to give. "The only explanation I can offer is that a portal has formed inside your front door because you wished it to."

Once again, Hugh looked deeper into the cottage. "Er, not to be dense. But *why* would I want a portal between realms behind my front door?"

Morpheus could only shake his head. "I'm afraid I cannot answer that. Perhaps you desired familiarity, and this is how your new powers chose to manifest it. Or perhaps it stems from your concerns about your ability to navigate through the veil unaided."

Iridaceae transformed, glancing around. "How does it work from the other direction?" she wondered, and went bounding off toward the back door. Hugh's cat meowed and trotted after her.

Hugh looked alarmed. "We should go with them. What if they get separated from us somehow?" He hurried to follow the pair.

Morpheus kept pace, swallowing the urge to explain that it did not matter if the familiars returned to the Night Lands without them. Given the unprecedented nature of what Hugh had apparently done here, perhaps caution was warranted until they had more information.

The back door stood open, still showing the familiar environs of Earth beyond. A light drizzle had set in, the clouds above low and gray. Iridaceae led the way, skipping excitedly through the damp grass as she circled the side of the structure. The front door was also open, just as they'd left it mere moments ago.

Hugh hesitated. "So, this will lead back to the Night Lands if we go inside? Is that how it works?"

"I do not believe so." Morpheus stepped inside the perfectly normal entryway, the veil slipping over him once more. He turned, and through the door he could see the rocky slope with its bubbling rivulet and ever-expanding plant life. Hugh, Iridaceae, and Baphometh were nowhere to be seen.

The others joined him from the area outside the front door in the Sublunary, reappearing in his vision as they entered one by one. Hugh turned, taking in the view of the Night Lands. The human swayed, steadying himself with a hand against the plaster wall.

He swallowed hard. "I... don't really feel so well all of the sudden," he said faintly.

Morpheus frowned, running silent calculations in his head. "In the Night Lands, the back door of the structure is encased within the mountainside. I hypothesize that the cottage behaves normally within the Sublunary unless one exits the front door. Similarly, within the Night Lands, once one enters through that door and passes through the veil just inside, exiting the structure by any other means—back door or windows—deposits one back on Earth."

Iridaceae tilted her head, eyes alight with curiosity. "Okay, but what if we're in the Night Lands and climb inside through a window? Baph?"

Baphometh darted out the front door and disappeared around the side of the cottage. Iridaceae went to open the window in the living area, which was not buried in the rock of the mountainside. A moment later, a black cat hopped up on the sill and leapt inside.

Hugh sat down rather abruptly on the battered green sofa.

"And you're saying *I* did this, somehow?" His voice sounded increasingly distressed as he raked a hand through his brown hair, clutching at the strands. "Morpheus, I didn't mean to do this! What if I do something *else* unintentionally? I can't... *how do I stop this happening?*"

Hugh's eyes had gone fever-bright, and as Morpheus watched, molten bronze kindled in their depths. The human's gaze locked onto his with stark desperation, the psychological break Morpheus had feared lurking far too close to the surface. Hugh's breathing came fast and ragged.

Without thinking, Morpheus crossed the few feet separating them and sank down on his knees. He took Hugh's shaking hands in his, cradling them.

"Leave us for a few minutes, please," he told Iridaceae and Baphometh.

"Yes," Iridaceae said. "Um. We'll just go and... catch some mice or something. Coming, Baph?"

Morpheus waited until she'd transformed and the pair had disappeared into the drizzle outside, then he turned his full attention to the man on the couch. Hugh's breathing hadn't slowed. If anything, it had grown even shallower and more uneven than before. His head moved slowly back and forth in wordless negation.

"Speak to me, my hunter," Morpheus said softly.

Hugh gulped — an ugly, choked noise.

"Morpheus." His voice was low and rough. "I can't be the thing standing between humanity and Phobetor. I know I said earlier that I thought everything was going to work out okay… but, I think that was just the water talking?"

Morpheus squeezed the shaking hands cradled in his sharply. "You are not the only thing standing between Phobetor and life in the Sublunary. *We* are, along with whatever allies we can gather."

Even to his own ears, it was scant reassurance.

Hugh gave a single bark of laughter, high and hysterical. "I punched the God of Fantasy in the face and it didn't even rock him an inch! Maybe I can't argue that this isn't happening, but it's going to be one hell of a long time before I'm anything other than a shitty little baby god!"

Releasing his hold on Hugh's hands, Morpheus surged up and pulled Hugh close against him, holding him tight as panic rolled off the human in waves. He wrapped one hand around the nape of Hugh's neck, the other arm circling his shoulders as Hugh's fingers grasped at the back of his robes, digging in like claws.

"I can't be the reason Phobetor wins," Hugh choked, the words muffled against Morpheus' shoulder. "What if I can't protect the Earth? What if I can't protect *you*?"

Morpheus drew breath to reply—however incorrectly—that he did not require protection. But he was interrupted when Iridaceae and Baphometh, both in human form, rushed into the room, only to slide to an ungainly halt upon catching sight of Morpheus wrapped around Hugh in a tight embrace.

"Erm… sorry," Iridaceae said. "Only, we thought you should know that something weird is happening."

Baphometh nodded in agreement, eyeing them uneasily. "You know those wards you and the fat bloke put up in the Night Lands? Well, for some reason, they're here on Earth as well."

"They're surrounding the cottage here, too," Iridaceae added breathlessly. "I think Hugh must have wanted the protection to work in both places!"

Still cradling the shaking human close, Morpheus raised his head as the implications of that began to filter in. "Did he indeed?" he asked, his tone brimming with speculation. He looked down at the top of Hugh's head. "I believe you are selling yourself short, my hunter. It appears your powers have a decided flair for both innovation and strategy, even subconsciously."

TWENTY-ONE

BEING A WET-BEHIND-THE-EARS godling was, Hugh reflected, surprisingly exhausting. After confirming that the cottage was warded both on Earth and in the Night Lands, Morpheus chivvied Hugh to bed in his familiar bedroom.

Hugh's sleep was suspiciously dreamless, under the circumstances—something which might have a tenuous connection to the fact that he awoke many hours later to find the God of the Sleeping Mind propped up next to him in bed, running smooth fingers through Hugh's tousled hair.

He blinked his eyes open, groggy with the kind of deep sleep that dragged at the muscles as well as the mind.

"Where're the others?" he slurred, feeling unaccountably responsible for the foul-mouthed sushi addict that had formerly been his pet cat.

"Exploring your realm in the Night Lands, to keep an eye on things as it expands," Morpheus said, pausing in his slow stroking of Hugh's scalp. "They are staying within the wards, and should therefore be quite safe."

Right. Because Hugh had magically transported his cottage to straddle the boundary between realms, with one door leading to each. As you do.

Despite his hours of rest and recuperation, the faintly hysterical feeling that had been plaguing Hugh ever since Baphometh's transformation returned with a vengeance.

"I just woke up, and I still feel like I need to wake up. Y'know. *More*," Hugh said plaintively.

"You may take it on my authority that this is as awake as it is possible for you to be," Morpheus informed him.

Hugh pondered that.

"Well, *damn*," he muttered.

"I propose we explore your ability to sense hope in the Sublunary and follow its pull through the veil," Morpheus said, as if it were a perfectly normal sentence.

"Um… okay?" Hugh smacked his lips, feeling as though something was off, but unsure what it might be. He frowned, exhaling through his mouth against a cupped palm. "Hang on. I was sleeping for hours. Why don't I have morning breath? My teeth don't feel furry."

He glanced down at himself, surprised to find that he was dressed in a belted green tunic over linen braies and fine hose—an outfit that would not have looked at all out of place in thirteenth century Bath. "Wait, *what*?"

"Why would you wish to have morning breath?" Morpheus asked, in evident confusion. "As to your clothing, you altered it in your sleep, approximately two hours ago."

Hugh opened his unnaturally fresh and clean-smelling mouth to pursue the matter further, paused, and closed it again.

"You know what?" he decided after a moment's thought. "Never mind."

Out of curiosity, he concentrated very hard on his clothing—watching in amazement as medieval peasant garb melted into the practical work clothes of a prosperous twenty-first century farrier.

Morpheus raised an eyebrow, running an appreciative gaze over him. "Perhaps you will revisit your gentleman's wardrobe from the eighteenth century at some point. I *was* rather fond of that period."

Hugh felt warmth roll through him in the wake of that assessing onceover, followed quickly by cool air. He flushed scarlet as he looked down to find that his clothing had dissolved completely, leaving him naked.

"Oh, now *this* could be entertaining," Morpheus practically purred.

"Don't you fucking dare," Hugh said, quickly returning himself to decency. Or, at least, to being clothed.

The last thing he needed was his lover randomly making him so horny that his clothing disappeared.

"Yes, you're quite right," Morpheus said, with the appearance of contrition. "I suppose this is hardly the time. Shall we see how your new instincts fare when it comes to travel within the mortal realm?"

◆

After checking on the familiars and informing them of the plan, Morpheus spent the rest of the day trying to teach Hugh how to travel through the veil with intent. At first, it went nowhere. Quite literally.

Only after Morpheus revisited his trick of taking Hugh's hand and 'leading' him to a place he already knew — repeating the lesson several times — did something finally click within Hugh's newly expanded awareness.

"Oh," he said, as his twentieth attempt at taking them somewhere led to him and his companion stepping out into a familiar field abutting a vineyard.

Several members of the Society of Ageless Pagans yelped in alarm, whirling away from the impressively large cauldron of mulled wine they'd been dancing around.

"You!" Sir Reginald exclaimed. "Where on earth did you two spring from?"

A pleasant, bubbly feeling welled up inside Hugh's chest as he took in the revelers. "Funny you should ask that," he said.

"Well, grab a couple of staffs and join the party!" Sir Reginald gestured to the others. "After the grand success of our previous adventure, we are hopeful that our rituals may summon another god!"

Hugh let the atmosphere of hope pour into him — not that he was sure he could have stopped it.

"Yes, you certainly are," he agreed, feeling a little bit dizzy with the sudden influx.

"And you certainly *have*," Morpheus said, a tad sourly.

Sir Reginald blinked at him for a moment before the penny dropped. A huge smile crossed his face. "Oh, I see! Ha, ha! I suppose we did summon a god, didn't we?" Then he sobered. "No offense, but we were rather hoping for one of the *fun* ones."

Hugh coughed, grabbing Morpheus by the arm before nightmare shadows could begin leaking from his companion's eyes. "Yes, quite," he said. "Well, uh, it's lovely to see you all again." He threw a thumbs-up toward the scrawny young man sporting a stylish toga in robin's egg blue this time. "Looking good, mate!"

Before the situation could degenerate further, he wrenched himself and Morpheus sideways through the veil. This time, they reappeared in a city square after dark. A large gathering of people carrying candles and signs written in Cyrillic surrounded them. The wave of hope that slammed into Hugh was larger than what had been generated by their pagan friends, but also somehow less celebratory.

"A candlelight vigil for peace," Morpheus murmured, unhindered by nagging linguistic barriers. "And rather an impressive one."

"Yes," Hugh agreed breathlessly. He looked around, taking in the spires of surrounding buildings topped by onion domes, many of them brightly illuminated with architectural lighting. "What is this place? Moscow?"

"Indeed, it is," Morpheus confirmed. "Red Square, to be precise."

"Wow," Hugh said inadequately, feeling increasingly drunk on the quiet hope surrounding them.

For the next several hours, they hopped from place to place, following Hugh's instincts. He was positively buzzing with newly absorbed power when Morpheus finally took him by the arm.

"Perhaps we should return to the cottage," he said. "We are still unsure of your capacity, and there will be time enough to continue our travels after you have rested more."

Resting was just about the last thing on Hugh's mind—although exploring Morpheus' newfound ability to get Hugh out of his conjured clothing held a certain amount of appeal. Especially with the way all of his freshly gathered hope felt like it was fizzing inside his veins.

"If you say so," he agreed.

It took three tries for Hugh to successfully get them back to the little house on the boundary of the Night Lands, since zeroing in on a particular destination was apparently a bit trickier than simply following the pull of human hope to someplace random.

When he finally succeeded, it was with a real flush of accomplishment.

"Well done, my hunter," Morpheus said. "It appears that you have a knack for—"

He was interrupted by the noisy arrival of an owl and a pussycat.

"You're back!" Iridaceae exclaimed. "Thank goodness. I wasn't certain how much longer we'd be able to stall them!"

Hugh looked back and forth between them. "Stall… who, exactly?"

"Visitors," Baphometh said grimly. "And let's just say, they ain't happy. Especially after we told 'em we couldn't let them past the wards."

"*What* visitors?" Hugh asked again.

"Well, the fat bloke, for one," Baph told them.

"Only he's got Thanatus with him!" Iridaceae added. Her expression soured. "And someone else, as well. Someone you're not going to be happy to see."

Morpheus went still, as though he was looking inward. Then his gaze snapped back to his surroundings.

"Phantasos," he said in a low tone. "What business could he have coming back here so soon—and with my uncle in tow, as well?"

Hugh consciously unclenched his fists. It was surprisingly difficult to do. "Guess there's only one way to find out, isn't there? So, let's go see what brings the Grim Reaper and the Gormless Twatwaffle to our doorstep on this fine evening."

TWENTY-TWO

HUGH COULDN'T DENY the hint of satisfaction he felt at standing across the barrier of warding from Thanatus and Phantasos, knowing that he alone held the power to let them in... or *not*.

"See?" Dionysus was saying. "It's just like I told you."

"The fact that someone warded a corner of the Night Lands does *not* mean that a new god is coming into existence." Thanatus delivered the pronouncement in a severe tone.

"That's what *I* said!" Phantasos crossed his arms petulantly, glaring at Hugh through the invisible protection surrounding his spring.

Hugh pasted on a pleasant smile. "Hello, you lot! Fancy seeing you here. To what do we owe the pleasure?"

Thanatus' dark gaze skittered over Hugh without sticking. He addressed Morpheus instead. "Nephew. We must talk. Open the wards and let us in. This is no time for games."

"I fear I cannot do that, Uncle." The words were dry as dust. "As this is not my realm, and therefore I do not hold the key. Perhaps you would care to address the person who does."

Hugh waved cheerily. "Let's try this again. Hello. Why the fuck are you here?"

Thanatus glared at him. Hugh got the impression that had he still been properly human, that glare might not have been good for his health.

"You claim ownership of this place? Do not be ridiculous. You cannot become a god. You are mortal."

Hugh's pasted-on smile stretched wider. "Am I really, though?"

Morpheus lifted his chin. "You yourself granted Hugh de Ferrers immortality, Uncle. To ignore that reality seems facile."

Thanatus scowled. "He is still *human*."

"Apparently, that's up for debate," Hugh told him.

The God of Death waved a dismissive hand. "If that is the case, then prove it. Lower the wards."

Hugh hesitated. There were two sticking points here. The first was that he didn't particularly *want* Thanatus and Phantasos inside his territory. The second was that no one had bothered to tell him how controlling the wards actually worked.

"Go ahead," Morpheus murmured. "Thanatus will not harm this place, and he will not allow Phantasos to do so, either. You felt the wards being constructed. The key to controlling them is within you."

Hugh sighed unhappily. "Fine. I guess we do need to talk to them properly."

Morpheus had said that no one could enter the wards without Hugh's permission. Hoping it really would be as easy as that, Hugh focused inward, feeling out the shape of the energy that was being drawn from the bubbling wellspring to power the defenses. He'd spent enough time worrying about the drain that it wasn't difficult to find the connection again.

"Let them in, please," he told the spring, picturing a door opening.

Just like that, the wards swirled like an iridescent oil slick on water, parting to reveal a clear oval. Thanatus stepped through with the air of someone expecting a trick. Dionysus and Phantasos followed.

Hugh relaxed, letting the doorway collapse in on itself.

"Elpis' realm has claimed its new custodian," Morpheus said with finality. "Now, you have clearly come here for a reason. Speak it."

Thanatus narrowed his eyes. "You overreach, nephew. Just as your brother does."

"Oi." Hugh took a step forward, his fists clenched. "What the hell has Morpheus ever done except try to stop Phobetor from destroying everything?"

Interestingly, Phantasos blanched at that—and Hugh was pretty sure it wasn't due to concerns over potentially being kicked in the bollocks. He paused. "What is it?"

Thanatus looked like he'd swallowed a lemon. "Phantasos has come to me with a rather disturbing report. In fact, we were talking about it when Dionysus showed up spouting his unlikely sounding story about a new God of Hope."

"What sort of disturbing report?" Morpheus asked in alarm, beating Hugh to the question.

Thanatus gestured vaguely toward Phantasos, as though the prospect of relaying the information himself was too wearying for words.

Phantasos chewed his lower lip like a nervous lad trying to drum up enough bravery to talk to a pretty girl at a maypole dance.

"*Well?*" Hugh barked, channeling the soldier he'd once been.

And Phantasos... *flinched*.

"Phobetor is fomenting a new world war," he mumbled, directing his words toward the ground. "Using those awful bombs that make everything poisonous afterward. The really big ones."

Morpheus inhaled sharply. A beat of silence passed, while Hugh's brain sorted through the words to make sure he'd understood them correctly.

He shook his head, trying to dislodge them. It didn't work.

"Phobetor's inciting a fucking *nuclear war?*" Hugh said, the words rising in pitch and volume until he was shouting. "What the *fuck*, Phantasos! Seriously... *what the fuck!*"

Phantasos flinched again, harder this time. "I came and told Thanatus as soon as I found out about it. This wasn't part of the deal."

He sounded like a sulky teenager, but now that Hugh really stopped and looked, there was fear in his eyes. *How Phobetor would love that*, he thought. *Oh, the irony.*

Too bad he had no room to talk. The implications of Phantasos' confession fell down on Hugh like shards of crumbling glacier, burying him in ice. Phobetor would have found plenty of sustenance from Hugh's burgeoning terror as well.

Beside him, Morpheus had gone very still. "He must be stopped. At all costs, we must prevent this."

Thanatus' lips thinned.

A horrible, nauseated feeling roiled Hugh's stomach. "You want him to do it," he realized. "You want the death."

He thought of the hunger for hope that had swelled inside him while visiting the peace vigil in Red Square. The way it had filled him up with bubbly warmth, better than the finest champagne. *Addictive*.

Christ. *The peace vigil*.

Had they been protesting against a coming nuclear conflict? Hugh hadn't looked at the news for… how long had it been? Days, at least. In the current climate of insanity, *anything* could have happened during that time.

He met Thanatus' gaze with a suffocating sense of desperation. "Look — I get it. I *do*. A war like that must sound like a banquet to you. But Thanatus, *think*! One glorious orgy of fear and death… except then it's all gone. *All* of it. *Forever*!"

"From out of the mouths of babes," Dionysus said under his breath.

"No more fantasies." Phantasos' voice held a barely hidden quaver.

"No more dreams," Morpheus said.

"No more drinking," Dionysus added. "No more sex. No more dancing."

"No more hope," Hugh whispered, and the realization ripped through him like the first mortal wound he'd ever taken, back on a nameless thirteenth century battlefield.

Morpheus stepped forward, staring up at his uncle. "Your lust for death does not outweigh your family's needs for the trappings of life."

Thanatus stared down at him, a thoughtful expression on his dark face.

TWENTY-THREE

"FUCK HIM," HUGH said frantically. "If Thanatus won't do the right thing, then *fuck him*. We have to act! What can we do? When and where is this war going to start?"

Morpheus appeared frozen… at a loss in a way Hugh had seldom seen before. Hugh turned on Phantasos, his hands clenching into fists at his side. He had to resist the burning urge to take another swing at the God of Fantasy's perfect face.

"You!" he snarled. "Tell us everything you know! Or, I swear to god—I mean, I swear to… *something*—I will rearrange those perfect teeth until the only people fantasizing about you will be *dentists!*"

Phantasos gulped, his usual cavalier attitude nowhere to be seen.

"*Well?*" Dionysus prompted. "*Talk*, lad! We don't have time for your ego!"

"There was a proxy war," Phantasos said hoarsely. His mournful gaze turned to Morpheus. "I didn't ask what it was about. I didn't *care*. But you saw one of the battles, when Thanatus took us to Phobetor to get your opal pendant back."

Something flared behind Morpheus' expression—memory, or understanding.

"This proxy war," Hugh pressed. "It got out of control somehow?"

Powerful nations had been hashing out their grievances against each other by destroying remote, less powerful nations for as long as Hugh had been alive. Those wars were bad enough in their own right, but the danger was always that things would spill out onto the wider world stage, like a controlled burn in a forest turning into a raging wildfire.

"It's about to," Phantasos said, sounding defeated. "An agent for one of the sides set off a bomb in the other side's capital. It killed the President's wife and children. And, you know, a few thousand other people. The group that took credit for the attack has open ties to the first side's ruling regime."

Hugh felt sick. "Are we talking about Russia and the United States here?" he asked, once again remembering the vigil in Red Square.

Phantasos shrugged. "Who else? They're the ones with the most bombs. Phobetor inserted himself as a close advisor to the American leader. He'll talk him into attacking Russia directly."

Hugh shuddered. If the man's entire family had just been killed…

"We have to go," he said, his pulse pounding fast and thready in his throat. "We have to go right now. But I don't know how to—" He broke off, shaking his head. "Where is the President now? Who knows how to get us there? Morpheus?"

"It will take time to find the dreams of a single person," Morpheus said faintly.

"Time we might not have," Hugh breathed.

Thanatus, who had been watching the exchange with a stony expression, spoke. "I must speak to someone about this." He paused, looking between Morpheus and Phantasos—still ignoring Hugh completely. "I will not attempt to stop you, should any of you choose to act in the Sublunary."

With that, his body dissolved into streamers of inky black, swirling away into nothing.

"Big of him," Dionysus muttered. He eyed Hugh, then Morpheus in turn. "I can't help you find this person. I've barely been on Earth in the last two thousand years, and I've never even heard of this '*America*'." One bushy eyebrow lifted. "But it seems to me that someone fantasizing about getting revenge by literally ending all life on the planet would stand out—" His attention fell on Phantasos. "—to certain people."

As one, everyone turned to the God of Fantasy.

For a moment, he looked like a startled deer frozen in the path of a lorry. Then, he let out a sharp breath.

"Yes," he said. "All right. Come to my palace. I'll get you to him."

Iridaceae and Baphometh had been skulking unobtrusively in the background during the conversation—not that Hugh could blame them. Now, they stepped forward.

"We'll come, too," Iridaceae said.

"No," Morpheus and Hugh said in unison.

"It's too dangerous," Hugh added.

"Stay here," Morpheus told them. "The wards will protect you, and neither of you can help with what is to come. If we fail, and Phobetor gains supremacy among the gods, this may be the only remaining safe place."

It was a brutal synopsis of what was to come. Both familiars flinched visibly. Baph recovered first, pulling feline indifference around himself like a cloak.

"Fine," he said, ostentatiously examining his fingernails. "We can tell when we're not wanted. We'll just stay here, then, won't we, Ir?"

Iridaceae sent Morpheus a fretful look, but she nodded.

"Stay outside the cottage," Hugh amended quickly, wondering with a horrible sinking sensation what would happen to a structure that straddled two realms, if one of those realms was destroyed in a nuclear holocaust. Would the wards on Earth's side protect it?

Baph gave a careless shrug of agreement and wrapped an arm around Iridaceae's shoulders, pulling her close against his side.

Dionysus cleared his throat. "Well. If this poor sod with all the bombs just lost his family, it doesn't sound like he'll be in the mood for drinking or fucking. I won't be any good to you on Earth, so I'm going to go try and beg an audience with Grandmother and Grandfather. Mostly because I'm worried Thanatus is doing the same thing right now."

Morpheus gave him a tight nod, and with a jolt, Hugh remembered that the celestial grandparents in question were *Chaos and Time*.

Fuck.

Dionysus' smile was unconvincing as he dipped his chin in a shallow bow. "Fortune favors the foolish," he said. "So, I imagine you three should be fine."

Then he, too, disappeared in a whirlwind of green leaves.

"Drunken arsehole," Phantasos muttered.

Hugh glared at him. "Yeah? What's *your* excuse, then?"

Phantasos sneered back, but somewhat amazingly, he did not return the verbal volley.

"Come with me," he said instead, and transformed into a swirl of gold flecks.

Morpheus, pale and wan, took Hugh's hand. Hugh stepped forward with him, emerging a moment later in a grand, gilded hall worthy of the embodiment of mortal fantasy. Phantasos was already there, muttering to himself as he paced around a massive, shallow receptacle full of liquid that glinted like mercury.

Rather than releasing Hugh, Morpheus squeezed his hand, guiding him around so they were facing each other.

"Hugh," he murmured, the words barely a breath. "You are not strong enough to face Phobetor alone."

"I won't be alone," Hugh pointed out, as though his body hadn't already ceded its private battle with fear. Clammy sweat dotted his upper lip, and his immortal heart felt like it was about to burst.

"I will stand at your side," Morpheus vowed. "Nothing will move me from my place at your right hand, my hunter. Perhaps Phantasos will stand with us as well. But dreams and fantasies will not influence a man bent on vengeance at the expense of an entire world. Only hope can counter that kind of fear, and your powers are, as yet, fragile and new."

Hugh's throat had gone tight and hot. "It doesn't matter. I'll *have* to be strong enough, won't I?" He knew how foolish the words sounded, even as he said them. "Not like there's really another choice at this point."

Morpheus drew breath to reply, but Phantasos interrupted.

"I have him. Stop bleating and get ready to go."

Hugh squeezed Morpheus' hand hard, trying for reassurance and probably coming closer to desperation. "Come on. We need to do this. It'll be okay. It has to be."

"Here, touch the edge of the reflecting bowl, both of you," Phantasos ordered. He held his hand hovering palm down over the rippling, mirror-like surface of the liquid contained within.

Keeping his hold on Morpheus with one hand, Hugh took a deep breath and let the fingertips of the other hand rest on the edge of the bowl. It was made of some gleaming golden metal—burning cold to the touch... or was it hot? Morpheus did the same, completing some invisible circuit. An instant later, the opulent surroundings of the Night Lands faded around them, replaced by rough concrete walls, harsh overhead lighting, and the suffocating feeling of tons of bedrock pressing down from above.

Hugh had a confused impression of a large oval table made of wood, with two people at the far end—one seated, one standing. He whipped his head around, finding Morpheus at his right shoulder, as promised... but no sign of Phantasos on his left.

The God of Fantasy had sent them on, electing to remain behind in the safety and comfort of his palace.

Irritation drew Hugh's lips back in a snarl. "That cowardly little arsehole!"

The seated figure at the table shot to its feet. "What is the meaning of this! How did you get down here?" said a gray-haired, portly man in a broad American accent.

His stick-thin companion, clad in a brown military uniform, turned slowly to face them. A slow, vicious smile stretched his pale lips.

"Ah, brother," Phobetor said, in his raspy voice. "How kind of you and your pet to join us."

TWENTY-FOUR

HUGH WASTED A PRECIOUS couple of seconds scanning the rest of the large room for threats. There were none. And that... didn't make sense. He might not be a dedicated student of American culture and entertainment, but he'd lived in this country once — for many years, in fact.

"Mr. President? Where are your bodyguards? Er, I mean, your Secret Service detail?" he asked, stepping forward.

There was no way in hell that the so-called *leader of the free world* should be down here alone in whatever underground bunker this was, with only Phobetor and an ominous looking black suitcase for company.

Hugh was trying hard not to think too closely about that suitcase, sitting open on the table with an antenna and square-edged, gunmetal-gray electronics peeking out. The phrase *nuclear football* floated through his mind.

"What need does the president have of security within his own impenetrable emergency operations center?" Phobetor asked, and Hugh shuddered at that all too familiar voice, like wind in dry branches. "There is no danger to him here."

"Well, *we* certainly got in without much trouble," Hugh pointed out.

Phobetor's thin lips pulled into a smile. His tone turned condescending. "Yes. As I said, there is no danger to him here. All the danger lies above." Green eyes flickered up toward the ceiling, with its oppressive mass of unseen stone and earth pressing down on their heads.

"Who are these people?" the president demanded, still on his feet. Shiny beads of sweat stood out on the man's forehead. Dark, baggy circles under his eyes spoke to some toxic stew of grief, lack of sleep, and the weight of the decision symbolized by that open suitcase lying on the table.

"They are unimportant," Phobetor said. "Mere unwanted distractions who have wandered in where they have no business."

With a start, Hugh realized that Morpheus' hand was still clutched in his. Slender fingers squeezed his in wordless encouragement—a reminder that this was on him, and no one else.

Hugh took a deep breath. "We're here to keep you from making a terrible, tragic mistake," he said.

At least the president seemed cognizant of what was happening. Hugh had been worried that they would find some mindless puppet, helpless beneath Phobetor's control. The man's bloodshot gaze flickered to the device containing the nuclear codes, his expression wavering between guilt and terror.

"*Mistake?*" Phobetor hissed the word like a snake. "The only *mistake* would be in allowing those who bombed innocent women and children without provocation to live. Indecision is the enemy here."

"There are innocent women and children in Russia, as well," Morpheus replied in that low, hypnotizing voice of his—the first time he'd spoken since they arrived.

"Innocent!" The president's Midwestern drawl thickened with passion. "Those useless sheep have had *decades* to overthrow that blasted regime of theirs! Don't talk to me about *innocent Russians* when it was one of them that killed my wife and my precious kids!"

"Yes, that's right," Phobetor crooned. "No one in the world will be safe as long as the war criminals survive. There's only one way to deal with America's enemies. Only one permanent solution to end their reign of terror."

Hugh could feel his hands shaking beneath the force of his shattered nerves—a mirror of the trembling president, who looked once again at the suitcase with something dangerously like longing.

"No!" Hugh argued desperately. "That's just not true! There can be a better, safer, and more just future—but not if you start a *nuclear war!*"

The president's eyes fell on him, wide and fever-bright. "Not a war, just a... *limited exchange*. Russia won't launch everything they have. We'll take out Moscow, and they'll destroy something in return to save face, and then the danger will be over! But if we don't show them that there are consequences—" He cut himself off and shook his head as though he was feeling dizzy.

"That's *insane!*" Hugh cried, stepping forward and letting Morpheus' hand drop. "That's not what's going to happen if you launch those missiles—you must *realize* that!"

Phobetor's smile hadn't wavered. "On the contrary, it's *exactly* what's going to happen, little creature."

Abruptly, those otherworldly green eyes loomed huge in Hugh's vision, taking over his entire awareness.

"Brother, *no!*" Morpheus snarled.

Distantly, Hugh felt the God of Dreams lunge forward, hands closing around his shoulder like claws... but then his perception of the outside world snuffed out like a candle flame. Just as had happened once before—long ago in an eighteenth-century alley—he was alone inside his mind with the God of Fear.

Bony fingers riffled through his thoughts and memories, leaving cold horror behind.

"Hmm... how interesting," Phobetor mused. "What manner of creature are you trying to become, little human? This hope is familiar, and yet I do not recognize its source. It does not belong to *you*, that much is certain."

Hugh clenched his teeth against the unbearable sensation of spider legs skittering beneath his skin. "Yes... it... *does!*" he grated, trying to channel Elpis' powers to defend against the panic fluttering at the edges of his mind.

Phobetor laughed, the sound like a wet cough. "You think so? Well, then, I suppose you should have guarded it better."

And with that, a wave of the worst terror Hugh had ever experienced swamped him, driving all thoughts of hope, of rationality, of *survival* from his head in the space of a heartbeat. He screamed, not sure if the sound made it past his lips and into the real world. All the horrors of death, the kind he had never truly experienced in eight hundred years of existence, permeated his body. Maggots squirmed. Worms feasted on decaying flesh until nothing remained but bones that dried and crumbled, reduced to dust by time.

Unmoored and blind with panic, Hugh's consciousness plummeted down and down and down, surrounded only by darkness. Until, finally, even the blackness disappeared, leaving nothing but an empty void.

———◆———

Morpheus lunged forward as Hugh's knees began to buckle, grabbing him by the shoulders. The sick, sinking feeling inside him followed him down as he cushioned Hugh's boneless collapse to the floor.

He had felt the moment Phobetor reached out with his mind, taking the battle to the psychic plane rather than the physical one. From the beginning, there had been a terrible sense of inevitability about this confrontation, and yet, Morpheus had stupidly told himself that they had a chance... that they might somehow prevail.

"Hugh, *fight him!*" he snapped, aware of how impossible a request that was. His lover had been a god for all of a day, if that — while Phobetor had been feasting on the mortal fear he'd created for *decades*.

Morpheus clutched Hugh's convulsing body, biting back a cry as blood and spittle flew from the human's lips. In mere seconds, the fragile form in his arms went rigid, muscles seizing. His subconscious awareness of Hugh's bright soul faded and slipped away like water held in cupped hands. He was left, not with the familiar, disconcerting monotone hum of Hugh's dormant consciousness whenever his body sustained injuries too great to survive.

Instead, he was left with... *nothing*.

The body he was holding went limp, its breath sighing out. Morpheus stared down at the slowly cooling, inert hunk of meat and viscera in his grasp.

Very deliberately, he settled the human corpse on its back on the floor.

Very deliberately, he rose to his feet.

Across from him, Phobetor had watched the drama unfold with a smug expression of victory. Meanwhile, the president had stumbled back a step, his simmering fear now hovering on the edge of full-blown, animal panic.

"Wh-what happened to him?" the human demanded, his voice shaking.

Morpheus, his own thoughts still mired in denial and disbelief, could not form words.

Phobetor, it seemed, had no such challenge. "Havana Syndrome. Clearly, the enemy has perfected their microwave weapons to work at great distances underground, and they are targeting this bunker. Quickly, Mr. President—you must act *now*, before a second attack neutralizes your ability to order the launch. Kill the perpetrators before they kill *you*."

Morpheus drew in a sharp breath at the lazy satisfaction lacing his brother's tone—the satisfaction of a predator with its prey trapped helplessly beneath its talons. He watched in horror as the American commander-in-chief lunged toward the mechanical device lying open on the table.

Unthinking, acting purely on instinct, Morpheus surged forward as well. One hand thrust out, his palm landing roughly against the human's forehead. Sick dread—both his own and his victim's—flooded his mind as he channeled his essence through the tenuous connection, doing the thing he had never before attempted to do, despite countless eons of existence.

Possessing the body of a mortal.

TWENTY-FIVE

THE VOID WAS not empty. It would have been far better if it had been. The fast-unraveling remnant of a soul that had walked the earth for eight hundred years had vague memories of having been in this place once before—but on that occasion, he'd been protected; his sleeping body safe in bed in the mortal realm.

Now, there was no loving god's embrace to shelter him from the sucking maw of rage and despair that reverberated within the Pit of Tartarus. The wails and growls of creatures unimaginably huge and unimaginably powerful awaited him below; monsters ready to snap him up like the most delicate of tasty morsels.

Terror washed through the remnant of Hugh de Ferrers in suffocating waves, each slow surge dragging away a little bit more of whatever ineffable flotsam and jetsam made a human being unique. It was so cold down here… colder than ice, colder than the grave.

It *burned*, that cold.

The shrieks of the angry Titans rose and fell around him—now rife with bottomless and never-ending fury, now mixed with mad, maniacal laughter. The noise vibrated through the pit, threatening to tear what remained of him apart until only subatomic particles and waves remained. The monsters' deafening roars were harbingers of entropy, ready to shred the tiniest clinging fragments of his being into randomness.

He fell like a doomed meteor streaking toward a planet, his guttering consciousness drawn as though by gravity to the only point of light in the unending nothingness of death—a tiny flame flickering like a beacon in the night.

A lighthouse on dangerous shores.

The impact jarred him to his core, for all that he crashed into the same nothing-space he'd been falling through moments before. The flame flickered huge in his awareness, a bastion of warmth in a frozen world.

Around him, the wild laughter rose even higher, before fading away to a low rumble of anger.

"You come to us for answers, Corpse Eater," came a voice like mountains shaking. "But your answer falls from the sky like a wounded bird."

In addition to the circle of looming creatures that were too large to comprehend, the remnant that had once been Hugh became aware of another presence nearby. This presence was different. Whereas the only rational reaction to the mad Titans was to *run*—if only he'd been able to do so—the other presence tugged at him like a magnet in the dark.

He tried to crawl toward it, but he was no longer a living thing with muscle and bone and sinew. His form felt like little more than a puddle, spread so thin that it would evaporate at the first touch of the sun.

"What is the meaning of this?" demanded a familiar voice.

Thanatus. Why was Thanatus here? Hadn't he gone to talk to... someone?

The God of Death leaned down, reaching a hand toward what remained of Hugh. His fast-dissipating form quivered, sensing the power of the deity who held sway over Tartarus and all its domains.

At the first touch, Hugh gasped, feeling himself coalesce into something with weight and substance. Not human… not living. But cohesive, held together effortlessly by another's will.

"You!" Thanatus said, in evident surprise.

The recent past filtered into Hugh's awareness in fits and starts. A war balanced on the press of a simple series of buttons. A terrified president, grieving the loss of his dead family and fantasizing about revenge. Phobetor, huddling off to one side like a stoop-shouldered vulture, waiting for his prey to succumb.

Morpheus' hand in his, clutching tightly.

Hugh drew breath to speak… but there *was* no breath. He had no lungs, no voice. He was dead, his personhood and agency lost forever. Fresh panic jolted through him.

"He stayed and fought," rumbled one of the Titans. "While you fled here in search of answers you do not deserve."

Hugh sensed Thanatus' surprise through the touch that was holding him together.

"He attempted to battle Phobetor directly?" the God of Death asked. "That is madness!"

"It is true, he had no chance of success," growled another of the Titans. "The odds against him were insurmountable."

A spark of stubbornness ignited inside the chest Hugh no longer possessed. *Insurmountable?* he thought mutinously. *I can't have lost. There's no one else!*

"Then why in fate's name did he do it?" Thanatus snapped, sounding inexplicably angry.

That earthshaking, mad laughter came again, rattling Hugh's nonexistent bones.

"Foolish little god," admonished the first Titan. "He did it because it's what Elpis would have done."

Thanatus sucked in a sharp breath.

The second Titan leaned in close, its single eye overtaking Hugh's flickering awareness. "Now it is *you* who must decide, Corpse Eater. Will you allow the new God of Hope to slip away in defeat, joining his predecessor in eternal nonexistence?"

Tension radiated from Thanatus, his grip on Hugh's insubstantial form tightening.

"What are you saying?" he asked, sounding unsure for perhaps the first time since Hugh had met him.

Now all of the Titans leaned down, looming over Hugh and Thanatus like mountains poised to tumble down on their heads.

"Your nephew—our Light-Bringer—is locked in battle with his fearmongering brother," said one of the Hundred-Handers, two of its chitinous legs scraping together like a chef honing a knife. "The fate of the Sublunary hangs in the balance. You hold the dregs of the mortals' hope in your hands. Will you allow it to slip through your fingers?"

Thanatus froze, clutching Hugh's tattered soul like one grasping a dangerous animal—unsure if it would be safer to hold on or let go.

———◆———

Morpheus clung to the American president's consciousness like a rider clinging to the back of a plunging steed. Mere milliseconds after he had made the desperate decision to control Phobetor's pawn directly, his brother had followed suit—battling for control of the frantic man's mind.

While this was the first time Morpheus had ever attempted such a maneuver, that was clearly not the case for Phobetor. Morpheus had first tried to send the man to sleep, but the president's terror—bolstered by Phobetor's presence inside his mind—prevented it.

Next, Morpheus had endeavored to paralyze the human with a nightmare. Again, Phobetor had blocked him, channeling the dream images into the perception of a waking threat. The president lurched unsteadily toward the open suitcase on the table, hands outstretched and shaking.

Battered by human stress hormones, Morpheus attempted to lock the man's muscles by brute force of will. But he had only recently escaped eighty years of captivity, and he'd been subsequently weakened by Phobetor's scheming attacks. By contrast, Phobetor had been feasting on mortal fear like a glutton at an endless banquet. For all his unimposing physical form, his brother's powers were stronger than Morpheus had ever known them.

Aware that he was fighting fire by pouring accelerant on it, Morpheus redoubled his efforts to swamp the human's mind with nightmares, feeling the mortal's heart thudding impossibly fast inside the man's chest. If he could push that heart hard enough, perhaps it would burst before Phobetor could get the president's fingers on the keyboard embedded within the black case.

A ragged gasp came from the floor, somewhere on the far side of the oval table, interrupting his concentration. From inside the human's body, Morpheus attempted to whirl. The harsh noise had come from the place where Morpheus had laid Hugh's empty, soulless corpse.

But Phobetor and the president were both resisting him, still straining toward the nuclear suitcase. And when the gasp from the floor was followed by a familiar, heartfelt groan, Morpheus lost control of the human's will.

Phobetor had ripped Hugh's essence free of his body and hurled it into the void. Morpheus had *felt* it. Hugh was *dead*. He could not now be waking… could he?

In his need to see, to *know*, Morpheus' focus slipped. Phobetor gleefully surged to the forefront, driving the human president to cross the final two steps and place his hands on the keyboard.

"No!" Morpheus cried, once more back in his own body. He lunged up from where he had collapsed to the floor during the attempted possession, thinking to attack the president with physical force.

Before he could do more than reach out, thick ropes of pitch-black voidstuff coiled around

Morpheus' arms and legs, pinning him in place as effortlessly as a parent holding back a flailing toddler. At the same moment, more tendrils whipped out, restraining Phobetor and the human president as well.

"*Stop*," came a deep, familiar voice, as the God of Death appeared before them. "You will both cease this insanity *at once*."

TWENTY-SIX

HUGH GROANED AND pushed himself into a sitting position, his arm muscles trembling like the legs of a newborn calf trying to rise for the first time. He'd been lying crumpled on a hard concrete floor, his legs hopelessly tangled and too weak to move.

Confused images of darkness, flame, and huge, monstrous creatures played across his memory in a jumble. Above him, Thanatus stood with his arms outstretched, tendrils of blackest night coiling outward from his hands.

"What's happening?" Hugh rasped, following the curling course of those tendrils to three people arrayed around the room.

Morpheus was the closest. "*Hugh*," he gasped, straining against the loops of darkness holding him immobile.

At the sound of that familiar voice, more of the recent past filtered in. Hugh's breath caught as he painfully rolled onto his knees, gaining a clearer view of the second figure standing nearby. The American President stood hunched over the edge of the large table dominating the room, his hands on the unseen mechanism inside the nuclear football.

"You! *Human!*" Thanatus said, his voice like thunder. "You have no *conception* of the death you are about to unleash! You have become a pawn of the gods, in contravention of our laws. If you still intend to take this action now that you are free of their influence, you should know the truth of what you will bring about."

With no more warning than that, the room around Hugh disappeared. In its place appeared a symphony of destruction so vile that Hugh nearly collapsed straight back to the floor.

Over and over, blinding light seared cityscapes across the globe, incinerating people and buildings alike. Farther from the impacts, blast damage crumpled trees and houses like an angry giant knocking over toy bricks. The dead littered the ground. The injured lay groaning, no one left to come to their aid.

Even farther away, humans and animals sickened as radiation shredded their cells from the inside. Hair and teeth fell out; eyes turned cloudy and sightless. Skin sloughed away. Tumors grew.

Ash filled the sky, circling the globe again and again. Temperatures plummeted. Crops failed. Famine spread across lands not already turned to volcanic glass, and Hugh shuddered at the visceral memory of gnawing hunger pangs that could never be sated.

The president let out a low moan of agony, his body still bent over the open suitcase. Tears poured down his cheeks, dripping from his sagging jowls.

"Uncle," Morpheus said, his tone full of foreboding. "*Stop this vision at once.*"

In the next instant, Hugh felt it, too.

The president was not responding to this prophecy of world destruction with rational trepidation. He was not experiencing the desire to prevent it happening by stepping back from the brink.

He was responding with terror.

Phobetor jerked fruitlessly against Thanatus' restraint, an evil smile cracking his thin lips.

"On the contrary, *Uncle*," he practically purred. "Let your vision run its course." His attention fell avidly on the trembling president. "You see it, do you not? This is what will befall your country if you do not act now to stop the aggressors! You must ensure that only the enemies of the United States suffer this fate. You have only seconds left to act—send the codes, or your country dies!"

The man at the suitcase stared at Phobetor as though hypnotized, his eyes nearly bulging out of his face. "I... I have to save them," he muttered, wrenching his gaze down to the keyboard beneath his fingertips as he began to type.

Hugh launched himself to his feet, ignoring the way the world spun around him, gray and foggy at the edges.

"No!" he shouted. "Please, you must *listen* to me! *There's a better way*!"

Terrified, bloodshot eyes leapt to him, the fingers on the keyboard stilling for a vital moment. Hugh dragged in ragged breaths, aware that he had only seconds to come up with a counter-argument to overcome instinctive, animal fear.

Morpheus, Thanatus, and Phobetor were looking at him as well—the first with hope, the second with skepticism, and the third with open loathing. Hugh swallowed harshly, trying to wet his throat.

All at once, the vision of a babbling spring spilling out of a mountainside overtook his sick dread, soothing it. He closed his eyes for the space of a heartbeat, trying to channel that feeling… to bring it into existence in this cold, underground room.

"There's a better way," he repeated, more calmly this time. "But you can only bring it about if you make a leap of faith. Do you believe that there could be a better future for everyone? Do you have hope that the possibility exists?"

The president's mouth hung open, his attention still trained on Hugh as though he held salvation in his outstretched hand.

"There is no *better future*," Phobetor sneered.

"Of course there is," Hugh said, not breaking eye contact with the man in front of him. "Of *course* things can be better than they are today. Look down at your hands. Look what you were about to do. Frankly, the bar for a better tomorrow is pretty fucking low right now."

Something strange was happening inside Hugh's chest. An unnamed force was flowing *through him*, somehow — originating from a tiny wellspring in an entirely different realm, and spreading outward through the room in gentle, lapping waves.

The U.S. President wrenched his gaze down to his hands, poised on numbered keys. He gasped and jerked away, staggering back a step.

"That's it," Hugh said, very calmly. "Let's say *'not today'* to a global nuclear holocaust, yeah?"

At which point, the trickle of power holding him upright and draining into the room around him dried up. Hugh's heart gave a worrying stutter, his lungs abruptly unable to draw breath. He wheezed, his knees going loose and shaky as though they'd suddenly remembered that he'd been dead a few minutes ago.

His eyes rolled up, and consciousness fled before his body even hit the floor.

<hr>

For the second time in mere minutes, Morpheus watched helplessly as Hugh crumpled, his consciousness fleeing. He jerked against his uncle's bondage, flooded with the need to go to the fallen God of Hope.

"What do I do?" asked the American leader. Tears choked his voice. "I don't know what to do!"

Thanatus' lip curled back in distaste. "You should do whatever you would have done, if not for the interference of deities."

Phobetor threw his head back and let loose a crack of laughter, even as Morpheus snapped, "That is *not helpful*, Uncle!"

"I don't understand what's happening to me," the president said unsteadily. "Have… have I been drugged? Am I hallucinating all of this?"

"No." Morpheus' tone was grim. "This is very, *very* real. Your actions will shape the future, for better or worse."

Despair settled over the man's craggy features. He gestured at Phobetor with a shaking hand. "But… General Timor is right. My family is dead; my country is under attack. There *is* no better future. What if destruction is the only way to get justice?"

"Destruction is the only way to get *revenge*," Phobetor said, with vicious relish.

And all at once, Morpheus knew what Hugh would want him to do, if only he were still conscious and able to speak. Throughout the confrontation with his brother, the only strategy Morpheus had been able to come up with was to fight with the weapons at his disposal.

Nightmare.

Possession.

Very nearly with tooth and nail.

He'd not only been fighting the wrong battle; he'd been doing it in completely the wrong way.

"Revenge solves nothing," he said, his voice growing soft. "And justice for a few does not negate fresh injustice visited on billions. Look inward instead. Dare to dream of that *better future*."

Closing his eyes, Morpheus followed threads of daydream into the human's mind. No darkness of nightmare flowed from his eyes like spreading shadows. Instead, he gathered the remnants of hope from the American leader's subconscious, twisting and plaiting them into a gentler dream of tomorrow.

No bombs flew. The candlelight vigils for peace, like the one he and Hugh had visited in Red Square, grew and spread like flowers blooming in springtime. The presence of tens of millions, *hundreds* of millions gathering to demand an end to the madness eventually pressured even the most radical regimes to come to the negotiating table.

With fear fading and sanity returning, the true cost of global war outweighed the unfettered need for more and more power. After all, what was gained by ruling a lifeless wasteland from within an underground bunker?

Morpheus could *feel* the dream taking root... gaining solidity in the president's consciousness.

The man sagged, collapsing into a chair and gripping the edge of the table with both hands. His head bowed, a wracking sob hitching his chest.

"Do you see it now?" Morpheus asked, in his most soothing tone—ignoring the flat, disapproving stare Thanatus was leveling at him.

The human's shoulders shook, tears trickling down his cheeks for long moments. Eventually, he took a deep breath and straightened his spine, dragging his composure together.

"I... yes. I'm not fit to serve," he said. "The grief... I think it's sent me over the edge. I'm hallucinating. I don't even remember why I thought I should come down here alone with *him*." His bloodshot eyes fell on Phobetor, accusing.

Phobetor glared back at him coldly.

The president gulped, a convulsive movement. "I need Harriet down here... the vice president, I mean. She should convene the cabinet. Make a motion to remove me under Section Four of the Twenty-Fifth Amendment."

"*Weakness*," Phobetor spat.

"Strength," Morpheus countered hotly. "The kind that you will never understand, brother." He turned back to the human. "Is there a communications device in this room? Can you contact your aides, your security detail?"

The president hesitated, then nodded. "I'll do that right now." He rose on shaky feet, crossing to a red telephonic device attached to the wall near a series of large, blank screens.

Morpheus held his breath until the brief exchange ended. It seemed to involve a fair amount of shouting on the other end. The man nodded and replaced the handset on its mount.

"People are coming down to help," he said in a blank monotone. "Or possibly to haul me away with a butterfly net, when they walk in on me talking to a roomful of my own delusions."

"Release me, Uncle," Morpheus said. "It is time for all of us to leave."

Narrowing his eyes, Thanatus withdrew the loops of voidstuff wrapped around Morpheus' limbs. "Yes," said the God of Death. "It most certainly is."

Morpheus was gratified to see that he did not immediately release Phobetor as well. His first concern, however, was Hugh. He barely noticed his uncle and his brother swirling into nonexistence as he dropped to Hugh's side, sliding an arm under his shoulders to lift his upper body.

Unlike last time, Hugh's chest still rose and fell. His heart still beat, weak and thready. His body still lived, but Morpheus could sense nothing from his mind. Not consciousness, not dreams, not the low monotone hum of his soul's hibernation during death.

The muffled sounds of clanking lift machinery heralded the arrival of more humans on the scene. Swallowing his disquiet, Morpheus spared a last glance at the defeated president, slumped once more in a chair — this time, one situated as far away as possible from the nuclear suitcase.

Confident that matters in the Sublunary were in hand — to the extent they could be, at least — Morpheus scooped Hugh's unconscious body into his arms. He rose, picturing Hugh's familiar cottage in his mind; hoping against hope that his lover retained enough divinity to slip through the veil with him.

TWENTY-SEVEN

MORPHEUS BREATHED A SIGH of relief when Hugh's body stayed solid and heavy in his arms as he stepped through the veil, emerging in the strange in-between space that the cottage now occupied.

He'd come directly to the bedroom, the bed-clothes still rumpled from the last time he had watched over Hugh's sleep. Trying to ignore the panic fluttering in his breast, he laid his burden down on the mattress and tugged sheets and covers over him.

Hugh remained deeply unconscious, unmoved by the familiar surroundings. Morpheus straightened, at a loss as to what he should be doing. Hugh had an understandable aversion to human hospitals. Even before he had spontaneously become a god, his immortal constitution put him at risk of ending up as a metaphorical lab rat if the medical profession discovered his seemingly impossible powers of recovery. Morpheus had personally presided over one such near miss in nineteenth century Edinburgh, and knew what was at stake.

"The water," Morpheus realized, immediately rushing toward the front entrance that led to Hugh's domain in the Night Lands. Drinking from Elpis' wellspring had bolstered Hugh's nascent powers once before. Perhaps doing so again could revive him.

Throwing open the door, Morpheus stared out in dismay at the withered remains of the plants and flowers that had so recently sprung to vibrant life.

The mountainside was unnaturally quiet. It took a moment for him to realize why that seemed so wrong—the sound of babbling water should have underpinned a background of rustling leaves and birdsong.

Now, everything was silent.

"No…" Morpheus breathed, stepping out of the cottage in a daze. Where a burbling brook should have flowed, there was now merely damp stone. The crack in the mountain that should have been the source did not so much as drip.

Elpis' wellspring of hope—*Hugh's* wellspring of hope—had gone dry.

"Morpheus!" Iridaceae's cry was high-pitched with panic. She came running up to him and flung herself into his arms. "What *happened*? Everything dried up and died! Baph is stuck as a cat again!"

Morpheus caught her, shamefully glad for the feeling of her strong arms around him. He buried his face in her short hair for a guilty instant, before steeling himself to pull back and meet her amber-colored eyes.

"Hugh channeled hope to prevent the American President from starting a nuclear war," he told her, straining to keep his voice steady. "Apparently, he channeled *all* of this place's hope. He is inside, unconscious. I cannot sense his mind or soul at all."

"Oh." Iridaceae looked taken aback. "It… worked, though? The humans aren't going to destroy everything?"

He wished he could offer a straightforward, definitive answer.

"Not today, it seems." He tried not to think about the implications if hope was truly gone forever from the Night Lands. If *Hugh* was truly gone forever.

"All right," Iridaceae said uncertainly. "Well, I suppose that's... good?"

"Better than the alternative, certainly," Morpheus agreed without enthusiasm.

Iridaceae frowned. "If Hugh is unconscious because he used too much power, would the water from this place help?"

"The spring has dried up," Morpheus said, although the fact was blatantly obvious to anyone with eyes. "There *is* no more water."

"There's the water Baph and I used to fill up your sister's jar when things started to go wrong," Iridaceae said, as though it was the most natural thing in the world. "The plants were dying, and the stream was getting smaller. We thought it might be good to store some, just in case. And the *pithos* was just lying around by the spring, so..."

She trailed off with a shrug.

Morpheus gaped at her, speechless for so long that she crossed her arms defensively over her chest and said, "*What?*"

He reached for her again, pulling her close and leaning down to press a kiss to her forehead. Then he straightened, meeting her startled gaze.

"You are the most intelligent and resourceful familiar that anyone could ever ask for," he told her, not breaking eye contact.

Bright pink flooded her cheeks. "Well, it was actually Baph's idea, before he became a cat again. But I *did* find the *pithos*."

"You are *both* amazing," he said. "Quickly, where is the vessel?"

"In the kitchen." Her gaze skittered away. "I know you said not to go in the cottage, but we thought it would be better. The water was disappearing on this side of the veil. We figured it might be protected if it was technically stored in the Sublunary, instead."

"Let us go and see," Morpheus said, not willing to entertain the possibility that the water in the jar might have disappeared with the rest.

He let Iridaceae lead the way, trying not to wince as she leveled a glare at the damaged pantry where he'd locked her in, not so very long ago, so he could commit suicide uninterrupted. Sure enough, the *pithos* with its veins of powdered opal stood on the counter next to the sink. Morpheus held his breath as he peered into the narrow neck, and let it out in a relieved gust of air upon seeing the shimmer of water within.

"It's still there," he murmured. "Thank the fates."

"You think it will work, then?" Iridaceae asked eagerly.

"I think that the fact we both feel hopeful about the prospect must certainly be a good sign," he replied.

She thought about that for a moment and shrugged. "Makes sense, I suppose. You have to carry it, though. I'd never forgive myself if I tripped and spilled it on the floor."

Morpheus repressed a shudder. "Prophets forbid."

He picked up the jar and returned with great care to Hugh's bedside. Baphometh, still trapped in cat form, had snuck inside while they'd been talking, and he was now curled up with his chin resting on Hugh's leg.

"Iridaceae says we have you to thank for this idea, my friend," Morpheus told the animal. "Let us see if your foresight will bear fruit."

Ever so carefully, he climbed into the bed next to his lover. Ever so carefully, he lifted Hugh's upper body to rest against his chest, supporting him in an upright position. Once they were settled, he grasped the pithos and held it to Hugh's slack lips with one hand, cupping Hugh's chin with his other.

It wasn't clear that Hugh was able to swallow, so Morpheus poured tiny sips of water into Hugh's mouth, massaging his throat in hopes of getting it into him properly. Every drop that trickled down Hugh's chin felt like an excruciating waste, but he tried to tell himself that even if it was merely touching Hugh's skin, it might still help.

It took more than an hour to get the entire contents of the jar into him, as much as possible. There was no change in Hugh's unresponsive state during that time, or during the hour that followed. Morpheus held him, Baph and Iridaceae watching avidly with him.

"I don't think it's working," Iridaceae said with obvious reluctance, as their vigil crept into the next hour. Baph gave a worried meow of agreement.

Morpheus dreaded what he was about to say, but as time crawled by with no visible improvement in Hugh's condition, his other responsibilities loomed ever larger.

"I must return to Tartarus and speak with Thanatus," he said, each word a struggle. "I fear that, left to his own devices, he will release Phobetor to do more mischief in the Sublunary."

Iridaceae looked scandalized. "He *wouldn't!*" But then, she hesitated. "Would he?"

"I don't think I dare take the risk," he said. "You two will look after Hugh for me, will you not?"

"Of course we will!" Her reply was immediate. "I can find you if there's any change." She chewed her lower lip. "It's just that he'll be worried if he wakes up and you're not here."

"I know." Morpheus reluctantly lowered Hugh's upper body to rest on the bed, placing the pillow beneath his head with care. "However, I would rather have him awake and worried than risk all his efforts by allowing Phobetor to continue his machinations on Earth."

Iridaceae sighed. "Well, yes. There's that."

"I will return as quickly as I can." Before he could talk himself out of leaving, he rose and focused on his uncle's palace, slipping through the tangled veil surrounding the cottage to emerge in Thanatus' throne room.

To his surprise, in addition to the God of Death and Phobetor, Dionysus was also present.

"Cousin!" Dionysus greeted. "Oh, good. You're here. How's our newest family member doing?"

Morpheus leveled a cold stare at Phobetor. "He is unresponsive. Saving the Sublunary from destruction depleted every bit of his power."

Phobetor only sneered at him. "Really? What a terrible shame."

Dionysus winced. "Oh, damn. I'm sorry, cousin. Perhaps he'll recover with time and rest. I could bring him some wine later, if you think it might help."

It couldn't hurt, even if a god's wine probably wasn't what Hugh needed to recover.

"Your thoughtfulness is appreciated," he said. "May I ask what brings you here? I did not expect to find you as part of this discussion."

A slow smile crept over Dionysus's broad features. "I was just getting to that part. You know how I said I needed to talk to some people?"

Morpheus frowned. "I assumed you were referring to the Titans. Were they helpful?"

Thanatus looked between them sharply.

Dionysus seemed surprised. "What? No… dealing with those monsters once a millennium is plenty for me, thanks all the same." His smile grew wider, gaining an edge. "In fact, I was begging an audience with our dear old grandparents. One which they eventually granted."

"*What?*" Phobetor hissed, even as Morpheus swallowed his surprise.

"Grandmother and Grandfather spoke with you?" he asked in disbelief.

"I find that hard to believe as well," Thanatus said, eyeing the God of Debauchery up and down.

Dionysus shot him an unimpressed look. "Yes, it's true. Our esteemed Kronos and Chaos do in fact deign to speak with their family members. At least, the ones who can be bothered to stop in and visit them occasionally." His hard stare moved to land heavily on Phobetor. "In fact, after I filled them in on what's been happening in the Sublunary, they're just *dying* to have a private word with you, cousin."

TWENTY-EIGHT

PHOBETOR'S GREEN EYES grew as wide as dinner plates. He lunged away from Thanatus' side, taking advantage of the fact that the God of Death had released the coils of voidstuff that had been holding him captive when they'd been in the Sublunary.

Morpheus threw up a hand without conscious thought, twisting reality to transform the flagstone floor beneath his brother's feet into a pit of glass marbles. Phobetor cried out as he stumbled, falling to his hands and knees as his footing shifted.

Thanatus growled in irritation and once more grasped Phobetor's limbs in loops of blackest night, holding him fast. Then his dark gaze fell on Morpheus, heavy and disapproving.

"I will thank you to stop damaging my castle, nephew," he said between gritted teeth.

"Forgive me, uncle," Morpheus replied, unable to muster much real contrition. "I acted before I thought."

With a final huff, Thanatus turned his attention back to Dionysus. "You spoke with Kronos and Chaos? Truly? I fear I will require your solemn word that what you have relayed to us is accurate."

Morpheus wasn't entirely certain what constituted solemnity from the God of Drunkenness. However, Dionysus was currently as serious as Morpheus had ever seen him.

He raised a bushy eyebrow. "I'm trying not to take offense at your implication, Thanatus," he said. "There is one simple way to confirm what I've told you, and that's to take Phobetor to see them, as they've requested. If I'm telling the truth, they'll be waiting for you. And if I'm not, then I imagine you were overdue for a visit with them anyway. They *do* get lonely, you know."

Thanatus still looked as though he suspected some kind of a trick.

"That logic seems quite unassailable," Morpheus said.

Thanatus' expression grew sour. "Then perhaps you'd care to join us, nephew."

But Morpheus only shook his head, his gaze for Phobetor alone. "No thank you. I have more *important* matters to attend to," he said dismissively.

Phobetor snarled at him, jerking against the bonds holding him.

"Very well," Thanatus said, in ill-tempered concession. "Come, Phobetor. Let us see what our esteemed ancestors have to say on the matter."

Morpheus watched, tense as a drawn bowstring, while Thanatus tugged his unwilling captive through the veil and disappeared. Then, his shoulders sagged.

"Thank you, cousin," he said hoarsely.

Dionysus patted him on the shoulder. "Don't thank me yet. Time and Chaos aren't exactly known for their predictability, I fear. But you should go back to your lover now. There's nothing more to be done on this end until our grandparents pass sentence."

Morpheus nodded, suddenly feeling as though his body weighed as much as a neutron star. "Yes.

You are correct on both counts. I will be in touch, Dionysus."

Dragging his too-heavy body back to Hugh's cottage felt like a herculean effort. Outwardly, it appeared that nothing had changed in his absence, either for the better or the worse.

Iridaceae and Baphometh looked up at his arrival; Hugh did not react.

"No change, I'm afraid," Iridaceae said. "What did Thanatus say?"

"Dionysus was there," he told her. "He spoke to Kronos and Chaos, and they have summoned Phobetor for… judgment, one hopes. They wish to speak to him about the matter, at any rate."

Iridaceae whistled, long and low.

Morpheus looked down at Hugh's unmoving form. "He's shown no improvement at all?" he asked, even though she'd as much as told him so already.

She shook her head sadly. "None. Now that you're back, I was thinking we should try to access his internet thingy. Maybe we can find out what's happening with the bombs and stuff."

Morpheus had given barely any thought to the *'bombs and stuff'* since returning here with Hugh's body in his arms—but she was correct.

"Yes. You are right; we should try to find out how the humans are reacting to their near miss. May I leave that assignment to you?" While Morpheus had gained a basic proficiency with the machine during his stint as a mortal, he still found it an awkward way to gather information.

"Sure." Iridaceae hopped to her feet and bounded off. She returned a short time later with the silver rectangle, setting it on the edge of the bed and lifting its thin screen, which flared to life with a photo of the Grand Canyon at sunset.

Morpheus settled himself at Hugh's side while she worked to open a web browser and search for current news.

"Things seem pretty crazy right now," she reported after a few minutes. "The American President has been removed, and the Russians are condemning his actions, claiming that he's solely at fault for the scare."

He nodded, not taking his eyes from Hugh's slack face.

"Oh," Iridaceae said.

That caught Morpheus' attention. "What?"

She frowned at the screen, poking at the keyboard. "People are gathering in the American capital. *Lots* of people. It sounds like what you said happened in Red Square. Only… bigger. *Much* bigger."

"They are protesting for peace?" he asked, an idea coming to him in disconnected fragments.

"Yes," Iridaceae confirmed. "It's happening in other cities, too. London, Paris, Tokyo, Mumbai, Islamabad, Cape Town…" She trailed off, her eyebrows rising toward her hairline. "Morpheus, I don't think hope is gone. I think it just… *moved*."

He caught his breath. "Hugh channeled hope from the Night Lands to the Sublunary. And now the humans are passing it from place to place within the mortal realm."

An ever-expanding wave—one that had over-whelmed its conduit.

His eyes flew to Hugh again. "I must take him back to Washington, D.C."

It was where Hugh had channeled his new-found power. Perhaps returning there would allow him to reclaim some small fraction of it for himself.

Baphometh meowed agreement.

"You should hurry," Iridaceae said, her brows furrowing in concern as she looked down at the unconscious man. "It can't be good for him to stay like this."

Hugh's cat hopped up on Morpheus' shoulder, draping himself around the back of his neck like a stole.

"I think Baph wants to go, too," Iridaceae said unnecessarily.

"Very well." Morpheus scooped Hugh's body up, taking care not to dislodge the animal from its precarious perch. "Perhaps you would care to join us as well?"

Iridaceae didn't bother to reply. She just trans-formed into an owl, staying close as Morpheus stepped through the veil and reappeared in the mid-dle of the National Mall with his three companions. They were surrounded by a press of people, all of them *singing*.

Iridaceae immediately flapped up, flying circles overhead. Morpheus wrapped a dreamlike aura around them, ensuring that no one in their immedi-ate vicinity would become alarmed at the sight of the unconscious body he held. The stately chords of a well-used gospel song echoed through the night, carried by countless voices in perfect harmony.

We shall overcome…

We shall overcome some day…

Just as they had in Red Square, thousands of candle flames dotted the darkness like a firmament of flickering stars. A comforting blanket of peace lay over the vast space, soothing the troubled waters of Phobetor's madness.

Morpheus closed his eyes, allowing the feeling to settle over him. Baphometh's purr rumbled against his nape. The whisper of Iridaceae's wings fluttered his hair.

In his arms, Hugh let out a slow sigh. Morpheus' eyes flew open, looking down at his lover — hope burgeoning in his breast. A soft groan escaped Hugh's parted lips. Among the warm press of humanity, surrounded by a song of aspiration for a better future, the still body cradled against Morpheus' heart stirred.

TWENTY-NINE

HUGH OPENED GRITTY eyes, his cheek pressed against warmth and his soul buoyed by music. "Where—?" he rasped, unable to make sense of the blurry points of light surrounding him in every direction.

"*Hugh*?" The familiar voice was breathless, and the body he was resting against shuddered with a trembling sigh.

"Morpheus?" Hugh blinked until a pale, worried face came into focus, gazing down at him. "What's happening? Where are we?"

Morpheus' face was limned with warm candlelight. His lips parted, but no words emerged… as though he was somehow overcome by emotion. Hugh tried to think back. The immediate past was a confusing smear of impressions, muddled like mixed paint. Fear. Urgency. And something sweeter. Something that flowed into him like cool spring water.

He drew in a sharp breath, recognizing that feeling for what it was. But that wasn't a memory. It was happening *now*.

Morpheus appeared to master himself after a moment. "We are back on Earth. Back in Washington D.C. The crisis, it seems, has passed."

For a moment, Hugh didn't know what crisis he was referring to. Then, it all came crashing back. His vision slammed into focus, the blur of light and darkness around him resolving into a massive crowd, many of them cradling candles in protective paper cones.

"A peace protest," he said, becoming abruptly aware that he was cradled in Morpheus' arms like a sleepy child. "Like Red Square."

He could feel the palpable aura of hope in a way he hadn't been able to, back then. It flowed into him—*through* him—like water through cracks in stone.

"The humans have chosen a side," Morpheus said, his voice hoarse. "They have thrown in their lot with you, rather than with my brother. These gatherings have sprung up spontaneously around the globe."

Shock suffused Hugh. "We won?" he asked, disbelieving.

He reached out with all his senses then, trying to feel what lay beyond this massive crowd singing their hope for a better future. But it didn't end. It ebbed and flowed, spreading wider, passed from person to person.

"We won," he breathed, not making it a question this time.

"I believe we did," Morpheus agreed, sounding equally awed.

As fresh strength suffused his limbs, Hugh once more became aware of his ignominious position in his lover's slender arms. A furry paw reached out and bopped him on the side of the head, making him flinch in surprise.

"Baph?" he asked, struggling to get down.

Morpheus allowed it, steadying him as Hugh got his feet underneath him. A black cat hopped from Morpheus' shoulders to his, claws digging in carelessly as he arranged himself on his new perch.

"I believe your familiar is tired of being trapped in animal form," Morpheus offered, as a tawny owl fluttered down to rest on his now abandoned shoulder. "But perhaps we should return to your cottage first. If you are quite recovered, that is."

Hugh tried to take stock. Good sense told him that he should be weak and ill with reaction after what had happened, but in fact, he felt as healthy and hale as he ever had.

"I think I'm fine," he said slowly. "Although I don't understand how."

A flicker of a smile passed over Morpheus's lips, not quite banishing the darkness lurking behind his eyes. "You gave hope back to them." He indicated the peaceful crowd pressing around them on all sides. "And now they return it to you a hundredfold."

Within Hugh, something settled, making its home between his lungs and burrowing in to stay.

"I've never felt like this before," he said in wonder.

"I daresay, neither have they," Morpheus replied.

⸺◆⸺

They returned to the cottage soon afterward. Dawn was breaking over this corner of the Night Lands. Hugh was appalled to find the oasis that had sprung up around his wellspring dead and rotting back into the rocky soil.

Both Baphometh and Iridaceae hopped down from their respective perches, transforming as they landed. Baphometh stretched his shoulders as though he'd been stuck in a cramped position for hours, looking around at the devastation.

"We couldn't stop it, Hugh," Iridaceae said mournfully. "We stored some of the water in Elpis' jar before everything dried up, and Morpheus made you swallow it. I don't know if that helped."

"Course it helped." Baphometh's tone was gruff. "He'll fix it soon enough, don't worry."

But Hugh couldn't reply. The barren landscape stabbed at his nerve endings like hundreds of tiny knives, trying to penetrate down to the freshly settled heart of him.

Morpheus' hand fell on his shoulder, a grounding weight. "This is your domain, Hugh. Its relationship with you is symbiotic. You channeled its power to stop the humans destroying themselves. Now you can channel power back to it."

Inside him, a tiny pool of spring water rippled. Wordlessly, he stepped away from Morpheus' touch, drawn unerringly to the place that had once been the source, but was now merely damp stone — cracked and crumbling. Reaching out a tentative hand, he tried to picture the water inside him calling to the water trapped beneath the mountain.

As though it was the most natural thing in the world, the spring burbled to life, first as a trickle, then as a gush. Clear water filled the meandering channel, and as Hugh watched, fragile new plants sprouted around its edges, tendrils curling outward.

"See?" Baphometh said, wrapping an arm around Iridaceae's slender form. "Told you."

The four of them stayed for hours as the sun rose higher in the sky—Hugh watching as the oasis bloomed once more, reaching beyond its previous borders with ever-increasing vigor. Meanwhile, Morpheus watched *him*, blue eyes never straying from Hugh as he wandered around the verdant area, crouching to touch a vine here or a cascading stem of flowers there.

Eventually, the God of Dreams stirred himself.

"I must find out what came of Thanatus and Phobetor's meeting with my grandparents," he said reluctantly. "The outcome of that discussion will greatly influence what we do next."

Hugh stumbled over the prospect of having to make yet more plans, only to catch himself on a memory. "Hang on. Your grandparents? As in…"

"Chaos and Time," Morpheus confirmed. "They summoned Phobetor into their presence, and Thanatus accompanied him."

"You think they'll punish him?" Hugh asked, looking up at his lover. "Or, at least, prevent him from doing the same thing again?"

"Unfortunately, one does not predict the actions of Kronos and Chaos with any degree of reliability," Morpheus said. "But I would feel better knowing what's going on."

"I'm right with you on that." Hugh rose from his position kneeling near the rushing water. "Okay, I think I can leave this place now. Shall we go try to get a report from someone?"

Morpheus squared his shoulders. "Yes. Let's."

And so it was that Hugh found himself being whisked off to a part of the Night Lands he'd never visited before, in the company of a pale, grim-faced god with an expression like storm clouds.

The domain of Morpheus' grandparents wasn't like any of the other places Hugh had seen in this realm. In fact, he had a feeling that if he'd still been human, it might have driven him mad in fairly short order. Trying to describe it seemed both pointless and impossible. It shifted from moment to moment, as though local reality held no meaning.

The closer they got, the worse it became. Even as a freshly minted god, Hugh wasn't all that confident he'd be able to continue. At least, not without puking up the spring water Morpheus had given him.

Hugh blinked, and suddenly Dionysus was standing before them.

"Hello! Bit like being drunk, isn't it?" He gave Hugh a sympathetic once-over and clapped him on the shoulder. "Come for an update?" he asked, his gaze flicking to Morpheus, who nodded.

"Afraid I don't have much for you," he continued, turning to look over his shoulder. "Thanatus stormed out a few minutes ago, muttering something about cleaning up other people's messes. Apparently, Grandmother and Grandfather kicked him out of the meeting, and now they're dealing with Phobetor in private."

"Well, that sounds promising, doesn't it?" Hugh asked.

"Perhaps," Morpheus allowed. "I suppose there's no hurrying Time. If you're willing to stay

here and monitor the situation, cousin, I should return to my domain to ensure that all is running
smoothly there. I hesitate to ask, but is anyone keeping tabs on Phantasos?"

Hugh had almost forgotten about the twatwaffle, but Dionysus only snorted.

"Holed up in his palace, sulking," he said.
"Don't worry—I think *he*, at least, has learned his
lesson."

Morpheus made a noncommittal humming
noise.

"Thanks, mate," Hugh said. "Let's the three of
us have a drink together when this mess is sorted.
Maybe I'll be able to keep up with you now."

"Ah, a challenge," Dionysus replied, a twinkle
in his eye. "I expect something can be arranged. It's
been too long since I hosted a proper festival."

Hugh wanted to ask what the hell he called the
last party where he'd drunk Hugh under the table,
but Morpheus was watching the exchange with that
faintly disapproving expression he often seemed to
wear when Dionysus was involved.

"Looking forward to it," he said instead, and let
Morpheus lead him away from the swirling chaos of
his grandparents' domain.

Only when reality reasserted itself in a recog-
nizable way did Morpheus grasp Hugh's arm and
whisk them to his familiar palace. But the echoing
throne room full of mirrors wasn't empty. Thanatus
paced restlessly back and forth among the gateways
leading to mortals' dreams.

At their arrival, he came to a halt, his spine stiff-
ening.

"Ah. Nephew," he said, sounding as though the words were being pulled from him one at a time. His eyes skated over Hugh without sticking. "It appears I am charged with assisting you in a task."

Morpheus, too, had drawn himself up stiff and straight. "What task might that be, Uncle?"

The God of Death looked like he'd just sucked on a lemon. "Phobetor has spent the last eighty years abducting your *oneiri* and releasing them as waking nightmares in the Sublunary. I am to help you retrieve them."

THIRTY

A MOMENT OF surprise warred with a surge of guilt in Morpheus' chest. His dream servants, the oneiri, were *his* responsibility. He had known, on some level, that their presence in the mortal realm was contributing to the madness, but he had not been in a position to address the matter, given everything else going on.

Hugh crossed his arms, tilting his head back to look down his nose at Thanatus. "Oh, so you're going to help retrieve them, are you? Sounds like Mum and Dad aren't too pleased with what's been going on in the Sublunary while you've been down in Tartarus, twiddling your thumbs."

Instinct urged Morpheus to rein Hugh in before he succeeded in needling the God of Death into real anger. He quashed the impulse. Thanatus still appeared completely unwilling to acknowledge Hugh's godhood. Cosseting his lover would do nothing to remedy that situation... and it *did* need to be remedied.

He waited, rife with tension, to see how Thanatus would respond.

"This has *nothing* to do with you, human," Thanatus snarled, looming over Hugh's smaller form.

Morpheus clenched his teeth against the protest that wanted to escape, forcing himself to let Hugh fight his own battles.

Hugh, who was apparently *more than ready* to fight his own battles, took a step forward until he was practically nose to nose with the older and more powerful god. Or, at least, nose to chin, given their difference in height. He reached a hand up and jabbed a finger into Thanatus' robed chest, not giving an inch.

"*Nothing to do with me*? What the *fuck*, Thanatus! News flash, but I just channeled every gods-damned ounce of power from Elpis' realm—from *my* realm—into the Sublunary to stop the humans destroying the *fucking planet*." Another jab. "So, *please do* tell me how this isn't my business, when I've been fighting on the front lines while you were busy sitting on your arse and waiting for Phobetor to send you millions of dead humans!"

And Thanatus… *stepped back*, as though he'd been *struck*.

Hugh looked as surprised as Morpheus felt, but he hid it quickly.

"Kronos and Chaos are deliberating Phobetor's fate," Thanatus said from between gritted teeth, looking back and forth between Hugh and Morpheus. "In the meantime, they wish for things in the mortal realm to be restored, as best they can, to how they were before."

"Hence your assignment to assist me with the oneiri," Morpheus said, with fresh understanding. Somewhat mollified, he shaped his next words into something more conciliatory. "Such assistance would be appreciated, uncle—there has been no time to address this aspect of Phobetor's crimes."

Thanatus was silent for a tense moment before accepting the olive branch.

"Retrieving them is a logical next step, I suppose," he said. "Such creatures were not meant for the waking world."

"No, they fucking *weren't*," Hugh agreed emphatically. "I've been a god for, like, five minutes… and even *I* know how out of line Phobetor was to break into Morpheus' domain and steal his servants."

Thanatus did not dismiss Hugh outright this time — which was, Morpheus supposed, progress of a sort.

"It is likely that the time spent in an unsuitable environment has twisted the creatures from their original purpose," his uncle said, directing the words to Morpheus while keeping a wary eye on Hugh. "Not all of them will be salvageable."

"I am well aware," Morpheus replied grimly, thinking of the rogue oneiri who had harried him during his stint in Hallucination, giving no regard to their former master.

"The broken ones will still have to be dealt with," Thanatus continued, with a hint of reluctance.

Morpheus knew what had put that faint tone of pity in his uncle's voice. Hugh, apparently, did not.

"What's *that* supposed to mean?" he demanded.

Morpheus steeled himself. "The oneiri are, in many ways, a part of me. Any that are too damaged or dangerous to return to the dream world will need to be destroyed."

Hugh jerked back from the words. "What? *No.* You can't just… *wipe out* parts of yourself!" He rounded on Thanatus again, his finger raised in warning. "That is *unacceptable*! Find a better answer!"

Thanatus sneered. "You think I *wish* to carry out this duty?"

"I don't actually give a shit about your *wishes*," Hugh snapped. "I'm telling you to think of something better! Look… let's just slow down and look at all the angles first, okay? If they can't be in the Sublunary, and they can't return to being dreams or nightmares, what *else* could the damaged oneiri do? Where could they stay instead?"

Thanatus' stony expression collapsed into a scowl. For a long moment, no one spoke.

Then he said, "Perhaps, with some adjustment, they could be repurposed to oversee the souls trapped in the Pit of Tartarus."

"You already have shades for that," Morpheus retorted, taken aback.

"Spending extended periods of time in the Pit isn't good for them," Thanatus said. "I must rotate them in and out, lest they disintegrate under the weight of the tormented souls' guilt."

Hugh looked thoughtful. "And that wouldn't be a problem for the oneiri?"

Thanatus looked sour. "As I have never attempted to place an oneiri in the role before, I am unsure how you expect me to know the answer to that question."

Hugh thought about that for a moment. "Fair," he said.

Morpheus turned the idea over in his mind, examining it from all sides. "Shades were originally mortal souls, subject to the same forces within the underworld as any other soul. The oneiri are my own creations."

"So, it's worth a try, is what I'm hearing," Hugh said. Then, grudgingly, he turned back to Thanatus. "Thank you for suggesting it."

Thanatus looked just as grudging as he replied, "As I said, I take no pleasure in the prospect of destroying the creatures. You were correct to demand alternative options."

Taking this temporary detente as about the best that could be expected, Morpheus gave a decisive nod. "Very well. If you are both amenable, perhaps we should go acquire a specimen and test your theory, uncle."

———◆———

It was pure chance that the first waking nightmare they came upon was the sniveling oneiri who had once tormented Hugh with dreams of his wife and child's death on a thirteenth century birthing bed, a small eternity ago.

"Let me go, *let me go!*" it squealed, its shadowy form twisting and writhing in Morpheus' hold. "You're not the boss of me anymore! *I ain't done nothing wrong!*"

"You don't belong here," Morpheus told it, looking around in disgust at the filthy political prison. Around them, groans of pain and fear emanated from behind the rows upon rows of heavy steel doors.

224

Upon their arrival, Hugh had taken one look at the place before letting out his own low noise of pain. He'd darted away from Morpheus' side without a word, and already, Morpheus could feel an invisible, fresh breeze of hope wafting through the stifling atmosphere of despair.

"*I was brought here!*" the oneiri cried. "When do I ever make decisions on my own? *He* made me come; *he* made me do this!"

It was slamming itself against Morpheus' restraint, as though it would tear itself apart if that was what it took to escape. Morpheus felt its pain like his own… felt the way it had been cut to ribbons and sewn back together wrong — its purpose lost forever.

"This one is broken," Thanatus said dispassionately. "It will do for our experiment."

Morpheus clenched his jaw, experiencing the oneiri's terror at the pronouncement.

"*No-no-no-no!*" it shrieked. "*I don't want to be an experiment!*"

For a terrible moment, Morpheus wondered if it would be kinder to destroy the creature after all. Then Hugh was at his side, a warm hand grasping his arm.

His lover looked gray with strain, but his expression was determined.

"Let me?" he said quietly, and turned to face the roiling mass of shadows. "Hey. It's not fair what happened to you. Not at all. But it doesn't have to be like this. You're really good at frightening people, I can tell."

Again, Morpheus felt Hugh's powers stretch out, surrounding them. The twisting, insubstantial form of the oneiri quieted, its attention focusing on Hugh as tendrils of hope wound around it. "I… yeah. I suppose I am." It paused, uncertain. "Hang on. I remember you. You tried to take my head off with a sword!"

Hugh stared at it, clearly taken aback. "I… what?"

"In a dream," Morpheus told him. "A very long time ago."

"Oh," Hugh said. "Right. Erm, sorry about that, I guess? I'm afraid I can be a bit of a stubborn arse sometimes. Still, I'm guessing it was only because you did a really good job of scaring me?"

"S'pose so," the oneiri muttered sullenly.

"Well, no swords today, for what it's worth. It just so happens I've got a job offer for you," Hugh went on. "Or, rather, *he* does." He indicated Thanatus, standing grim-faced nearby. "And we think you're going to absolutely *love* it, mate."

Morpheus watched, the tight knot in his chest easing as the oneiri uncurled from its defensive hunch.

"Yeah?" it asked. "You think? So, exactly what kind of job are we talking about, here?"

THIRTY-ONE

HUGH RAN A weary hand down his face, trying to banish the throbbing ache in his skull. Rounding up all the oneiri that Phobetor had stolen from Morpheus' domain seemed to take an age, but Morpheus and Thanatus had shown no hint of needing a break until their mission was complete.

Now, the pair were in Tartarus, attempting to complete the transformation that would allow the damaged creatures to perform their new function under Thanatus' care. The first oneiri they'd caught had ended up acting downright enthusiastic about the prospect of harrying souls bound for punishment in the Pit. After observing it for a while, Morpheus had declared the experiment a success, and they'd returned to Earth to capture the others.

Hugh knew, intellectually, that this was good news. The nightmarish creatures would no longer be able to spread terror in the mortal realm, and Morpheus wouldn't have to suffer the pain of destroying them. Win-win.

The problem was, every single time they'd captured one, it had been in a hell-hole of fear and despair. Hugh's need to offer hope to the humans stuck in those terrible places felt like an unbreakable compulsion—but it drained him more with every new location they visited.

The first time he'd stumbled over his own feet in exhaustion, Morpheus realized what was happening and insisted that they alternate hunting the rogue oneiri with visiting places where Hugh could replenish his power. Hugh doubted he could have continued to function without those periods of respite, but he was painfully aware that he was slowing the others down.

If any part of this mess could be said to possess a silver lining, it was that Thanatus had finally seemed to accept Hugh as the new God of Hope. In fact, it had been Thanatus who insisted Hugh continue to accompany them, despite the added delay of gathering fresh hope between trips.

"No," the dour God of Death had told Hugh, after he'd suggested letting the other two go on without him. "Your talent for convincing the broken oneiri that a better future exists may be all that is allowing them to move forward into their new responsibilities. You should stay with us."

Morpheus, who looked tired as well, had arched a brow in silent satisfaction and seconded the sentiment.

Now, however, the other two had retired to Thanatus' realm to finish the process. Before leaving, Morpheus took one look at Hugh and told him to stop overexerting himself and get some rest.

In theory, that had probably been good advice. In practice, Hugh couldn't imagine resting while so many people in the Sublunary were without hope.

Morpheus had told Hugh that being the god of something meant being the nexus of a series of systems. Unfortunately, as far as Hugh could determine, any systems governing hope in the human realm had fallen to pieces millennia ago. And he didn't have the faintest clue how to build them again from scratch.

Once more, he was a stereotypical medieval peasant, fruitlessly trying to extinguish a fire in a burning village by running back and forth to the pond with a bucket. He knew, on some level, that he should be trying to figure out how to invent fire-trucks and water pumps instead. But to do that, he'd have to put down the bucket, even though things were still burning.

And he couldn't bring himself to do it.

He'd just come from a village in North Korea where the entire population was dying of starvation, and he was trying to replenish his strength by visiting the dedication ceremony of a new school building in rural Burkina Faso. The longer he kept at it, though, the more imbalanced everything felt.

Worried that the area around his spring in the Night Lands might be wilting again, he willed himself back to the cottage to check on it. Baphometh was waiting for him, his arms crossed in disapproval.

"Don't say it," Hugh said tiredly.

Baphometh raised his chin with feline stubbornness. "Say what? That you're doing too much too fast and you need to *fucking stop*?"

"Is the spring all right?" Hugh asked, not replying directly.

"Are *you* all right?" Baphometh shot back, without missing a beat.

Frustration boiled over, despite his best attempts to stop it. "No, I'm not *fucking* all right!" he shouted. "Humanity is on a collective suicide watch, and I need to *fix it*! But instead of fixing it, I'm stuck here getting backtalk from my fucking *cat*!"

He shoved past Baphometh before guilt over yelling at him could start to set in, throwing open the front door. Outside, the landscape of vines and flowers that had sprung up around the waters of Hope were looking decidedly wilted, but not actually dead yet. He closed the door, leaning his forehead against the painted wood for a moment. Then he pushed upright on aching arms and braced himself to wade back into the fray.

"You can't rebuild Rome in a day, you idiotic twat!" Baphometh called after him, as Hugh clenched his jaw and stepped through the veil, aiming for the biggest void of hope he could sense.

———————◆———————

The next time he returned to check on the wellspring, it was Iridaceae who met him. She frowned at whatever she saw in his face, putting her hands on her hips in a way that somehow managed to radiate disapproval.

"I'm going to fly down to Tartarus and tell him what you're doing," she threatened.

"I don't have time for this," Hugh said, and headed back to the Sublunary with another metaphorical bucket of water.

This time, it was a city somewhere in South America where the children had been infected with a virulent new strain of yellow fever. Immediately, he was struck by a brick wall of hopelessness — parents watching their future die in the throes of seizures and uncontrolled internal bleeding.

Hugh doggedly channeled power from the waters of his domain, ignoring how sluggishly they had begun to flow. It felt like his bucket had sprung a leak, though. However much he channeled, it simply soaked through the cracks of despair that riddled the makeshift hospital ward where he was standing, unobserved in the shadows.

As another parent wailed in grief and collapsed weeping over the body of a dead child, the futility of what he was trying to do abruptly overwhelmed him. He fell to his knees with a gasping sob, clutching at his chest.

He would have collapsed flat on his face, but a presence materialized at his side between one labored breath and the next. Strong arms caught him.

"Enough," Morpheus said, in a tone that brooked no dissent. "Hugh, *enough* of this."

As easily as an owner scruffing a wayward kitten, Morpheus whisked them back to Hugh's cottage, which was thankfully empty of interfering familiars. Hugh wanted to jerk away… to round on Morpheus and berate him for interfering.

He drew breath to shout, only to choke on it and crumple forward instead — collapsing against a slender frame that always seemed to hold far more strength than it should be capable of.

"I have to fix it!" Hugh said plaintively, the words muffled against a wiry shoulder. "What the hell kind of god am I, if I can't fix the one thing I'm supposed to have power over!"

Morpheus was silent for a long moment, holding him.

Then, he spoke, his voice quiet but serious. "Shall I send every mortal creature to sleep for all eternity, then?" he asked. "Should Dionysus ensure that everyone on Earth is drunk for the rest of their lives? Or perhaps we should have allowed Phobetor's plan to go forward, so that Thanatus could reap the souls of every mortal thing at once."

Hugh stilled, not sure what he was trying to get at.

"Well… no," he said thickly, his throat clogged with unshed grief. "But that's different. I'm the God of *Hope*—"

"It is *not* different," Morpheus interrupted. "We are all the god of something. It is only when the balance is lost that things begin to fall apart."

"The balance *was* lost!" Hugh said.

"Yes," Morpheus agreed, not releasing Hugh from his embrace. "But it will not be restored by destroying ourselves in a misguided attempt to right things by brute force."

Hugh trembled with the need to protest, even as the truth of the words settled beneath his skin.

"Do you trust me?" Morpheus asked.

Hugh squeezed his eyes shut. "Of course I do."

One hand came up to tangle in the hair at Hugh's nape. "Then trust that we will restore the balance together, even if it does not happen tonight."

The fight went out of Hugh all at once, and he sagged in his lover's hold. "Promise?" His voice sounded painfully young for someone who'd watched the centuries slide past like raindrops rolling down a window.

"I promise," Morpheus said. "But first, we rest. I will not allow you to return to the Sublunary until your domain has recovered its power."

After a slight hesitation, Hugh nodded, not raising his head. "Okay." For the first time, he registered Morpheus' exhaustion as well as his own, and it occurred to him that the God of Dreams might be nearly as drained as he was, after so long chasing and recapturing the shattered pieces of himself.

"Good." With that, Morpheus urged Hugh to his feet. "I know it is difficult, my hunter. But hope only exists with hopelessness as a contrast. All will once again be as it was meant to be... eventually."

Allowing himself to be led toward his bedroom, Hugh could only hope that *eventually* would come soon enough.

THIRTY-TWO

MANY HOURS LATER—if time could truly be counted in such a way on the border between the realm of humans and the realm of gods—Hugh opened his eyes.

He blinked up at the familiar ceiling of his familiar room, the cracks in the plaster still unrepaired after the bomb that had gone off in Lower Ilham. Idly, he wondered if he could somehow fix those cracks just by thinking about it *really hard*, in the same way he could apparently change his clothing with the power of his mind.

Deciding that it might not be a good idea to start playing around with reality inside a structure that was balanced over an unprecedented portal between dimensions, he rubbed a hand over his face and sat up.

At some point, Morpheus had left, leaving Hugh alone in his rumpled bed. Worry pricked at him for an unpleasant instant, but some new awareness in the back of his mind hummed wordless reassurance that all was well. Taking stock of his body, he decided that he felt… better? Or at least, he felt a bit further away from a full-on physical and emotional breakdown than he had when Morpheus had dragged him back here last night.

He didn't think he'd been *asleep*, as such. In fact, he wasn't entirely certain he still *could* sleep, in the way normal humans did. Even so, whatever quiet, mindless state of relaxation he'd achieved in Morpheus' arms clearly counted as rest.

With an ironic burst of hopefulness, Hugh rose from his bed and shuffled to the cottage's front door. When he opened it, the landscape it revealed wasn't much changed from the last time he'd checked it. The oasis around the wellspring remained sadly wilted, its leaves mottled with sickly brown and yellow spots.

I will not allow you to return to the Sublunary until your domain has recovered its power, Morpheus had told him, in a tone that warned it was no idle threat.

For long moments, Hugh wavered between panicky desperation over the idea of countless millions of humans still laboring without hope, and shaky relief at the knowledge that he would not be allowed to hurl himself back into the maelstrom while his powers were so weak.

Humiliatingly, relief won out.

While it was true that Morpheus had also been weakened, he was still far stronger than Hugh. If he didn't want Hugh to return, then Hugh would not be returning. The decision was out of his hands.

The low thrum of someone else's lazy satisfaction threaded through the depths of Hugh's mind. He frowned, attempting to trace that thread to its source. In the end, though, there was really only one person it could be.

There were also a limited number of places where a god might have retired to amuse himself while his lover remained insensible with exhaustion. After confirming that the kitchen was unoccupied, Hugh went down the hall to the bathroom, with its antique, claw-foot tub and on-demand tankless water heater.

Here, he'd bathed a battered Morpheus after retrieving him from the collapsed bunker that had been his prison for eighty years. Here, he'd wrapped an arm around newly mortal shoulders, as Morpheus puked his guts out after sacrificing his godhood to save Hugh from the realm of Hallucination. Here, he had held Morpheus tenderly in the steaming water while they hashed out the details of their messy relationship.

And here, indeed, lay a porcelain-skinned god, reclining in the bath with his eyes closed and his dark head thrown back... the picture of decadence.

"Oh, good," Morpheus murmured, not looking up. "Worship is so much more restorative when more than one person is involved."

Instantly, Hugh was thrown back to that terrible, wonderful night when he'd hauled Morpheus out of his imprisonment—so weak he could barely stand unaided. *It appears your attentions are restorative*, Morpheus had said, after Hugh worshipped his body for hours... wholly unaware of the implications, for a god.

At the memory of exactly what form that worship had taken, Hugh felt himself harden so fast he was momentarily lightheaded. And, because he'd made precisely zero strides toward controlling his impulses in this regard, it was no surprise to find that he was now abruptly and comprehensively naked, when he glanced down at his own body to check.

"Bugger," he said tiredly.

"If you like," Morpheus replied in an absent tone, unhelpful as ever.

There was a faintly breathy quality to that velvet voice. It made Hugh look twice... and *keep* looking as Morpheus slid down in the bath, disappearing beneath the surface of the water with an enigmatic little half-smile.

Hugh crossed the short distance from the door after closing and locking it behind him. He was rewarded with the sight of his lover lying relaxed on the bottom of the tub, the fingers of his right hand sliding lazily up and down the length of his perfect cock.

Teasing himself, and no doubt fully aware of the show he was putting on for a worshipful audience of one.

"*Jesus fuck*," Hugh croaked, quickly squeezing the base of his own throbbing erection as it gave a warning pulse.

With what he thought was impressive foresight, Hugh grabbed a towel from the rack and threw it on the floor next to the tub, so he wouldn't be kneeling directly on the hard tile. Then he sank down to watch with avid eyes as the God of Dreams languidly pleasured himself, unhindered by the pesky mortal need to breathe.

While Hugh would have been content to drink in that sight for hours, his cock wasn't nearly so patient. When the urge to ease the pressure by rutting into his own fist grew nearly overwhelming, he channeled it into something more productive, instead. Reaching an arm into the tub and covering Morpheus' graceful hand with his rough one, he took control over the lazy rhythm of self-pleasure.

The lithe body in the bath arched as Hugh sped up his strokes, adding more pressure and swiping a thumb over the delicate pink glans on every up-stroke. Taken by surprise, Morpheus stretched upward toward the light and air. With his heart and dick thudding in double-time, Hugh stopped his ascent with a single fingertip on his forehead. He held Morpheus an inch away from the surface, working both their hands around his cock for several long seconds before gently pressing him back down to the bottom.

Morpheus went willingly enough, a slow trail of bubbles exhaled between his lips as he sank. His raven-dark hair floated in a halo around his head like the fronds of a sea anemone. Emboldened, Hugh guided his lover's hand away from its grip on his own prick, lifting first one arm and then the other to stretch up the back of the tub.

Spying Morpheus' discarded dressing gown on the floor next to the bath, he tugged the soft fabric belt free and used it to tie his captive's wrists loosely to the exposed plumbing—symbolic bondage that wouldn't have stopped a determined sparrow, much less an ancient deity.

Morpheus twisted against the light restraint for only a moment before subsiding, apparently content to be bound… at least in this context. The ripples on the surface smoothed, revealing another little cryptic smile. A moment later, gills morphed into existence on either side of Morpheus' neck, their delicate filaments waving in the current as water rushed past them, in and out.

"Brat," Hugh accused, unable to stifle his amusement at this new game. Diving back in—so to speak—he took over the work of jerking Morpheus' hard cock with one hand. With the other, he gently covered Morpheus' throat, folding the gills shut and holding them closed.

Morpheus writhed, the smile falling from his face as his lips parted in surprise. Blue eyes slid shut, dark brows furrowing. The hard flesh encircled by Hugh's other hand pulsed… betraying its master's pleasure at being symbolically dominated in such a way.

A god could not drown. But Morpheus had been reduced to mortality once. He'd also been enthusiastically complicit in a rather memorable sex dream of Hugh's—one involving a sea monster and the tide coming in. At the very least, he understood the concept of empty lungs from a theoretical standpoint.

Hugh, who felt he still owed Morpheus some payback for the sea monster thing, settled in to remind him what really mind-blowing sex felt like.

Deciding on the goal of seeing how many times in a row he could make Morpheus come, he alternated loosening his grip on the newly grown gills for a second or two, and pulling his victim up to the surface for a gasped half-breath every few minutes. Hugh took *particular* pleasure in cutting off those increasingly desperate gasps with a searing kiss that immediately pressed Morpheus under once more, newly breathless.

The feeling of water rushing past his fingers as Morpheus breathed through his gills was bizarre, and vaguely fascinating. In the end, Morpheus lasted only until the third kiss before his body jerked out its first release, tendrils of white semen swirling in the water around his cock. His bound hands gripped the exposed pipes almost hard enough to bend them before slowly going slack. His spent prick flagged for only a moment before surging back to hardness under Hugh's continued ministrations.

And so, Hugh kept doing what he'd been doing.

The problem with pleasuring a god—if you wanted to call it a problem—was that Morpheus presumably could have kept going like this for the rest of eternity. Hugh lost count sometime around the thirteenth wrenching orgasm. Some minutes later, he was taken by surprise when Morpheus snapped the fabric belt tied around his wrists with a sharp jerk. Abruptly, strong hands grasped Hugh by the shoulders and dragged him into the tub with a mighty splash.

Hugh let out a yelp of shock. After a few seconds' confused wrestling for position, he ended up straddling Morpheus' slender chest. He braced one hand on the edge of the tub, his bodyweight pinning his lover under the water. After a bit more tugging and manhandling to position Hugh to his satisfaction, Morpheus angled his face forward—still without bothering to come up for air—and swallowed Hugh's aching erection down to the root.

Hugh let out a cry that was nearly a roar. Warm water sloshed around him as demanding hands gripped his arse cheeks; urging him to thrust deep into a willing mouth, over and over. He would have happily shot his load down that tight throat… but at the last moment, the strong hands pulled him away and flipped them both over.

Hugh flailed, straining upward as Morpheus settled astride his torso, bracing himself with a hand over Hugh's heart.

He knew, intellectually, that he was no more likely to drown than Morpheus was. He was a god now, too… which didn't mean he was quite ready to test that theory in practice yet.

This was not, however, what Morpheus seemed to have in mind. While there was a playful threat implicit in the hand pressing down on Hugh's sternum, there was a different promise — not playful at all — in the way Morpheus slid backward, lining himself up and sliding down onto Hugh's cock.

Despite the absence of oil or lube, Hugh sank effortlessly into warm, welcoming heat; slick as wet silk. He groaned as the perfect sensation overtook him, all his muscles melting into a warm puddle.

Water streamed from the impossible gills on Morpheus' neck as he hummed his satisfaction. A moment later, the slits melted back into his flesh as though they had never existed. The graceful body impaled on Hugh's cock began to move in a slow, sinuous rhythm, and Hugh was lost.

When it finally came, his climax felt like pressurized lava erupting — burning his flesh with unbearable pleasure, rather than pain. The sensation flowed outward from someplace deep inside him… perhaps the same place where hope bubbled up from the depths of the Night Lands.

"Oh, *god*…" he choked out, as the welcoming passage wrapped around his cock fluttered and pulsed, milking every last drop of spend from his balls.

"Mmm," the god in question purred, his tone one of pure satisfaction. "Yes. You are *quite* welcome, my hunter."

As the aftershocks faded, Morpheus slithered down to lie pressed against Hugh's side within the relatively narrow confines of the antique bath. Hugh soaked up the tranquility and the intimacy of it in equal measure, drifting peacefully for an unknown amount of time until the cooling bathwater penetrated his awareness.

With a small noise of discontent, he nudged his companion's shoulder until Morpheus sat up.

"Can gods still get pruny fingers and toes?" Hugh asked.

His companion smirked. "Only through force of habit, I would imagine."

With a resigned sigh, Morpheus lifted himself gracefully out of the bath, the water sluicing off him and leaving him completely dry in its wake. Clothing reformed around his body, as neat and precise as ever.

Hugh followed suit, only with considerably less grace and considerably more lingering dampness. Not willing to trust his clothing choices to a sex-addled brain, he scooped up the now-beltless dressing gown and shrugged into it.

"Something feels different," he realized, grasping the robe around his waist. "I need to check on the spring."

Morpheus raised an eyebrow and followed him wordlessly to the front door. It opened to reveal an oasis, perhaps not in full bloom, but no longer beset by wilt and dying leaves.

"Ah," Morpheus said, decidedly smug. "*Much* better."

Hugh stared out at the verdant garden in consternation. "Hang on… what just happened?"

Morpheus tipped his head, watching hummingbirds dart among the vines and branches. "Worship can travel in both directions, my hunter," he said.

Hugh shook his head. "But… that doesn't make any *sense*. It usually takes concentrated hope for this place to get stronger!"

Full lips pursed in muted amusement. "Perhaps I *hoped* that such an interlude would help." He stepped closer, their shoulders brushing. "Clearly, more research is needed into the phenomenon."

Hugh peered at him suspiciously. "Is this your way of saying that we need to have crazy god-sex more often?" he asked.

"Your words, not mine," Morpheus replied. "Now, however, I believe it is time to discuss more sustainable ways for you to fulfill your purpose. The Sublunary needs its God of Hope hearty and hale."

Hugh sighed, resigned to the necessity of rethinking his approach to helping the humans. "Yes, yes. I suppose you're right… on both counts."

THIRTY-THREE

IT WAS WITH a sense of relief that Morpheus watched Hugh take a metaphorical step back over the following days, reassessing his approach to restoring hope in the human realm.

An unexpected secondary benefit came in the way Hugh's predicament made Morpheus reexamine his own duties with a fresh eye. Morpheus had not become a god. He had always been one. His function had been intertwined with his existence since he had emerged from his parents' union—Nyx and Somnus, Night and Sleep, combining to form Dreams within the collective unconscious of mortal creatures.

Now, he was forced to examine the *why* and *how* of godhood, so that he could assist the new God of Hope in reestablishing the framework of his power in the Sublunary. Hugh had confided that he felt like a peasant fighting a raging fire with a leaky wooden bucket full of pond water. He had asked Morpheus to help him figure out how to build fire stations and sprinkler systems, because, as he'd put it, "There's no fucking way that Elpis was doing this much work with this little effect."

And so, Morpheus had delved into the *whys* and *hows;* even going so far as to consult with Dionysus and Thanatus on the matter. The breakthrough had come when Hugh began to truly understand what had happened inside that underground bunker, with a grieving president poised over a black suitcase full of death.

Hope was not a finite resource that Hugh could only dole out from his wellspring in the Night Lands. Instead, hope was a virus, passed from carrier to carrier through acts large and small. Hugh's job was to manage the spread, ensuring it traveled through the populace efficiently, reaching all corners of the humans' world.

By restoring hope to one man, he'd ultimately restored it to millions, when the news broke that nuclear war had been averted. His job, as a deity, was not to sprinkle hope onto individual people from his tiny bucket. Rather, it was to identify the choke points, where Phobetor's ascendency had broken down existing channels of hope by introducing fear into key individuals and systems.

"Oh, this makes so much more sense now," Hugh had breathed, his eyes turning molten bronze with power as he'd looked inward.

Since then, Morpheus hadn't caught him draining himself to the point of collapse again. Baphometh had muttered, "*About bloody time*," and promptly turned into a cat, further reassuring Morpheus that the worst was over.

That left him to return his focus to his own domain. While he still felt a measure of guilt over allowing his stolen oneiri to terrorize the Sublunary for so long, the solution Thanatus had proposed for those that could not be rehabilitated appeared to be working admirably. The God of Death reported that his shades were healthier now that they were no longer required to work in the Pit of Tartarus. Additionally, more of the souls trapped there were choosing to move on, after engaging with the repurposed oneiri.

He supposed it made sense. Nightmares were not truly intended as torture for sleeping minds, but rather as signposts pointing the way toward self-knowledge. Perhaps that quality also lent itself to the guilty souls of the dead. Once their guilt was understood, some of them seemed to find it easier to transcend.

Still, despite his knowledge of the value of nightmares, with the smaller number of oneiri now available to him, Morpheus quietly decreed that pleasant dreams should take precedence. It was the best—and perhaps, the *only*—method at his disposal for fighting the aftereffects of his brother's reign of terror.

With Hugh engrossed in his own work, and things relatively under control in the realm of dreams, Morpheus found himself left largely to his own devices. Solitude had been his preferred state for such a long time that it felt odd to crave company.

When a presence swirled into existence at the entrance to his palace, however, it was not remotely the company he'd been hoping for.

"Hello, brother," Phantasos said cautiously, looking as though he was ready to flee again at the first hint of a cold welcome.

◆

Taken by surprise, Morpheus faced his brother in silence, fighting an internal battle. His first instinct was to throw the God of Fantasy out on his proverbial ear. Or, possibly, his literal one.

However, Phantasos had helped them in the end. If they hadn't been able to locate the American president quickly enough, it was quite likely that the Earth would now be little more than a heap of radioactive slag. While his brother had still chosen the coward's way out by sending them into danger and staying behind in safety himself — he had still helped save the mortal world.

"What do you want, Phantasos?" he asked, maintaining marble stillness in the face of his visitor's obvious nervousness.

Phantasos cleared his throat.

"I've come at Dionysus' behest, to deliver an invitation for you and your hum — " He caught himself and flushed. "Your... consort."

"Have you," Morpheus said flatly.

The flush deepened — a pretty pink stain over perfect cheekbones. "Yes. He's organizing a celebration on the morrow, at dusk. He wishes to see you both there."

"And he sent you to deliver this message... because?" Morpheus prompted.

Phantasos stood stiff and unmoving for the space of several heartbeats. Then, a gusty sigh deflated some of the tension in his spine.

"Because he wishes me to attempt to make amends with you, I would imagine."

Morpheus tilted his head, curious. "And is that something you feel inclined to do, brother?"

Expressive brown eyes slid down and to the side. "I know I made... poor choices."

After a moment to contemplate that grudging admission, Morpheus replied, "I cannot disagree. However, I am rather curious as to why. Have I treated you so poorly, that you would wish such terrible things on me and mine?"

Phantasos' gaze flew to him, only to slip away again almost immediately.

"I resented you," he mumbled.

Morpheus could only stare at him. "For the fates' sakes, *why?*"

His brother's jaw worked, as though he were trying out words, only to discard them. Eventually, he squared his shoulders and held Morpheus' gaze.

"Our functions are so similar," he said slowly. "And yet, mine is ridiculed while yours is celebrated. To have *big dreams* is lauded as worthy and ambitious. Yet those same people will dismiss my gift as *just idle fantasy*. As though I am nothing more than a time-waster."

Morpheus continued to stare, open-mouthed. After a moment, he caught himself and clicked his jaw shut with a snap.

"*That* is why you stood by while I was imprisoned for eighty years, and assisted in a scheme that nearly brought about the downfall of the Sublunary? Because the humans do not respect fantasy sufficiently?"

Phantasos nodded.

For a long moment, Morpheus found himself lost for words.

"Brother," he managed after several seconds, "every work of art, every piece of literary fiction, and a decent percentage of human procreative acts spring from your power."

Phantasos' expression wrinkled in consternation. "Well… yes. *I* know that."

Morpheus matched him frown for frown. "But you were… what? Upset that people didn't say it often enough?"

"As I said, I made poor choices." Phantasos sounded defeated. "And now, I don't know what I can do to atone, as Dionysus so clearly wishes me to do. Fantasy is important, but it won't fix things in the mortal realm the way hope will."

Morpheus wrestled with his response, balancing his own resentment with the needs of the wider world. He, too, let out a sigh.

"You are powerful, brother," he said. "Perhaps more than you know. It is likely that by tying your gift more closely to fear than to hope, you shifted the balance in Phobetor's favor." He held up a hand to forestall Phantasos' reaction. "I do not say that to accuse you. Rather, to point out that by allying with myself and Hugh—and, dare I say it, with Dionysus—you may help tip the balance back toward its point of equilibrium. I, for one, would consider that a form of atonement."

Phantasos appeared to mull his words over before replying. "I suppose that makes sense. Perhaps our sister's realm abuts both of ours for a reason."

Morpheus raised a pointed brow. "Not our sister's realm any longer," he said mildly.

"No." Phantasos let out a slow breath through his nose. "Indeed not. Our new God of Hope has grown much stronger than I expected, in such a short stretch of time."

"He had little choice in the matter," Morpheus said. "He is also infuriatingly stubborn. He would, however, benefit from your assistance. Perhaps I'll even discourage him from punching you in the face again when you offer it."

"How very kind of you, brother," Phantasos said sourly.

THIRTY-FOUR

"DO I NEED to go punch that smug little arsehole in the face again?" Hugh demanded. His left hand had clenched into a fist, seemingly without his volition.

"*No*," Morpheus said firmly. "In fact, I specifically reassured him that I would discourage you from such an action."

With a grunt, Hugh relaxed his posture and uncurled his fist. "So, he wants to *atone* now, does he? How nice for him."

Morpheus didn't need to read his companion's wistful daydreams of breaking Phantasos' perfect nose to detect the skepticism in his tone.

"As much as it pains me," he said, "we need him as an ally. As he himself pointed out, there is a reason your realm borders his as well as mine."

Hugh's expression—already sour—turned even more so. He let out a put-upon sigh and rolled his eyes skyward. "Fine. Yes. My life would be a lot easier if more humans were fantasizing about nice things, instead of fantasizing about revenge."

"My thoughts exactly," Morpheus agreed. "Now, tell me how you are faring. I haven't seen you for almost two days, and I daresay you are due for a rest. Even if that rest involves indulging in my cousin's excesses of food, drink, and dance."

"You forgot the orgies," Hugh added dryly. "Which, I should add, I'm happy to sit out. The private ones are so much more fun."

Morpheus covered a smirk.

"To answer your question," Hugh went on, "I wouldn't say things are *under control*, exactly. But at least I don't feel completely incompetent anymore. I think the tide in the Sublunary is turning, finally."

Morpheus gave a single nod. "I concur. Progress is slow, but the dreamers are less tormented than they were."

A fond smile tugged at Hugh's lips. "Well, you did stop sending them nightmares. The innocent people, anyway. Don't think I didn't notice."

Morpheus felt himself unaccountably flustered by that smile. He cleared his throat. "It was only logical, with so many of my oneiri now serving elsewhere."

"Mm-hmm," Hugh agreed. "And of course, it had nothing to do with your desire to ease suffering in the mortal realm."

"Merely a happy side effect," Morpheus said. "Now, though, we should be going, if we are not to be late to Dionysus'... *event*." He couldn't help the faint note of disapproval that crept into his tone, even if it was largely habitual at this point.

Hugh let out a laugh. "You sound like you're being dragged to a funeral rather than a party. Come on, I'll make it worth your while."

With a look of concentration, he waved a hand down his body. The simple peasant clothing he'd taken to wearing when he was in his own realm melted into something more refined—fitted tan breeches and white stockings, a white linen shirt worn beneath a tailored fawn waistcoat and knee-length jacket, the ensemble topped by an intricately tied cravat. His hair plaited itself into a short queue at the nape of his neck, tied in place with a length of black ribbon.

"Your eighteenth-century garb," Morpheus said, surprised and pleased. "I approve."

"I thought you might," Hugh said, unconsciously drawing himself upright, in the bearing of a gentleman. "Shall we, then?"

"I suppose we must," Morpheus said, long-suffering. His gaze sharpened. "As long as you are aware that I will be much less tolerant this time, should I find you passed out in our host's embrace."

Hugh winced, though amusement played around the corners of his eyes. "I'm banking on my newly acquired godhood standing me in better stead when it comes to holding my wine tonight."

"Hmm," Morpheus hummed, noncommittal.

———◆———

They arrived in Dionysus' domain to find that the God of Drunkenness had outdone himself. Almost immediately, Morpheus detected a slightly different atmosphere than during their last visit—a sort of ethereal euphoria that he barely recognized, so long had it been since he'd felt it.

Next to him, Hugh looked around the great hall, obviously enchanted. He, too, must be feeling the effects... even if he had no way to recognize the feeling for what it was.

Dionysus approached, his arms outstretched in welcome—broad and booming as ever. "Cousin! Hugh! *Welcome!*"

Morpheus accepted an embrace, along with the associated waft of alcohol and sex. "Hello, cousin. You appear to have enlisted an ally. I didn't realize this occasion was to be organized jointly with my brother."

The soft-edged sparkle of fantasy clung to the walls, the furniture… the very air around them.

Dionysus had enveloped Hugh in an embrace as well. At that, he pulled away and let out a hearty laugh. "Well, he didn't think you'd have come if you knew! Really brings back the good old days, doesn't it?"

"I suppose it does," Morpheus allowed.

Hugh gazed around with interest. "Huh. Well, I guess I can't punch him in the face *now*, can I? If he's one of the hosts, that would just be rude."

"Would it not be rude, regardless?" Morpheus asked dryly, and Dionysus laughed again.

"Go on, enjoy yourselves, you two," he said. "I need to go check on those S.O.A.P. people. They're absolute menaces with a lute."

Hugh gave a startled snort of amusement as he left. "He dragged the Society of Ageless Pagan folks here? Oh, gods, we're doomed."

"Perhaps we can avoid them," Morpheus suggested. "My brother's influence means that the celebration will become whatever an attendee wishes it to be. I suspect our tastes differ enough from theirs that we will be safe."

"Really?" Hugh said. "*Interesting*. Well, in that case, let's go find a chamber orchestra with some incredibly stuffy and intricate cotillion dancing."

And so, they danced, breaking at intervals for wine and conversation. Hugh was deep in a discussion with a satyr wearing a fine tailcoat over his naked goat legs when he tensed, his attention caught by someone's approach.

Morpheus immediately recognized Phantasos, excusing himself from his own conversation with a nymph whose expertise in astronomy rivaled her skills on the dance floor. Despite Hugh's earlier assurances, he made his way to them as quickly as politeness allowed—ready to step between them should it become necessary.

The pair had come to rest in a wary standoff.

Hugh eyed the God of Fantasy up and down, taking in his ornate pastel robes.

"Phantasos," he said flatly. "I guess we have you to thank for the party tonight, as well as Dionysus?"

Phantasos appeared just as stilted. "That's right. It seemed the least I could do, after… well, *after*."

"Yes," Hugh said, his voice still a monotone. "I agree that this is just about the least you could do."

Phantasos' expression clouded with irritation, but he smoothed it immediately. "I suppose I deserve that, don't I? But I didn't come to talk to you about the party."

"No?" Hugh asked. "What did you come to talk to me about, then?"

Phantasos appeared to steel himself, as though for something unpleasant. "I owe you an apology. More than one, in fact. While I understand that apologies don't change what happened in the past, I think it would be in the mortals' best interest if you and I could overcome our differences so we can work together."

Hugh blinked.

"Oh. That's…" He trailed off. Tried again. "That's… probably true. What, um—what did you have in mind? Exactly?"

Phantasos licked his lips, a nervous tell Morpheus had rarely seen from him before. "The thing is, I still have no memory of our sister Elpis. I assume she and I collaborated, but I don't know in what fashion. So, I suppose… we'd just have to play it by ear?"

Morpheus watched Hugh mull that over, struggling past personal dislike in favor of what was best for the mortals under his care.

"I see," he said at last. "All right. Why don't we discuss it in more detail sometime soon, when I'm not drunk on Dionysus' wine?" His brow furrowed in thought. "In fact, why don't we bring Dionysus in on it, as well? All four of us have complementary powers. Or, at least, we could do."

Phantasos gave a cautious nod. "Very well. I'm amenable to that."

"Good," Morpheus said with finality. "I will send Iridaceae to make the arrangements sometime tomorrow."

"*Late* tomorrow," Hugh put in.

"Sometime late tomorrow," Morpheus corrected. He frowned. "Speaking of which, where *is* Iridaceae?" He knew she was here, as was

Baphometh. But he hadn't seen either of them for quite some time.

Phantasos waved a dismissive hand. "She's having sex with that horrible cat-creature in one of the alcoves in the back. I saw them on my way over."

"Oh," Morpheus said, relaxing. "I suppose that's all right, then."

Hugh, by contrast, looked thoroughly taken aback. "Oh. Um, okay… wow. I know you ancient Greek gods are all about the weird hybrids. But I have to ask—what does a cross between an owl and a pussycat even *look* like?"

Phantasos shrugged. "I imagine it's either a cat with wings or an owl with a cat's head."

Hugh opened his mouth. Closed it. Thought about that for a moment.

"You know what?" he said. "Forget I asked."

◆

The celebration raged on, growing progressively more raucous as the attendees grew drunker. Morpheus found himself increasingly desiring a graceful exit. He was about to suggest as much to Hugh when a sudden stir at the hall's entrance drew their attention.

"Hang on," Hugh said, growing immediately tense despite the wine he'd consumed. "What's *he* doing here?"

Morpheus turned as well, to find the God of Death striding through the throng—a looming, dark-robed figure pulling a second, cowering figure along behind him.

"Wait. Is that—?" Hugh asked.

"It is," Morpheus replied grimly, as the pair made a direct line through the crowd toward them.

His uncle came to a stop in front of them both, the party having grown quiet around them. Low, speculative murmurs buzzed through the great hall.

"Morpheus," Thanatus greeted tersely. "Hugh."

"Thanatus," Hugh said, eyeing the God of Death's companion with clear misgivings. "Don't take this the wrong way, but what the bloody fucking hell is *he* doing here?"

Morpheus straightened to his full height. "I'd quite like an answer to that, as well, uncle."

Behind Thanatus, Phobetor cringed and tried to turn away, his green gaze sliding hither and thither in an attempt not to make eye contact with anyone in the room. Thanatus' implacable grip on his upper arm held him in place.

It was so unlike his brother's normal behavior that Morpheus looked back to his uncle in consternation.

"Kronos and Chaos have passed judgment," Thanatus said, his hold never wavering as Phobetor curled in on himself and tried to jerk free again. "They wished you to know their decision."

Hugh was still vibrating with tension, his full focus on the cowering figure, as one might focus on an unpredictable predator. "And what *was* their decision?"

Thanatus' lips pressed into a thin line. "For the next ten thousand years, they have decreed that

Phobetor will experience the fear he creates firsthand, rather than feeding on it."

Phobetor whimpered.

Morpheus' stomach performed a strange dip and roll.

Hugh sucked in a sharp breath. When he spoke, his tone was vicious. "*Good*," he snarled.

It took a moment for Morpheus to gather himself enough to speak calmly.

"That seems like… a surprisingly just and measured response," he said. "Thank you for informing us."

"Yeah," Hugh agreed, still with that angry snap in his tone. "Thanks. Oh, and Phobetor?"

Phobetor writhed in Thanatus' hold, refusing to meet Hugh's eyes.

"*Boo!*" Hugh surged forward, both hands jerking toward Phobetor's face.

Phobetor cried out in terror, renewing his attempts to break free.

"Very mature," Thanatus said tartly.

"And much less than he deserves," Hugh said, thoroughly unrepentant. "So, yeah. Thanks again. But I suddenly find myself with the urge to get out of here. Morpheus?"

"I couldn't agree more." Morpheus caught his uncle's dark gaze and held it. "I trust we have all learned something from this immensely unpleasant interlude."

Thanatus raised an eyebrow. "Yes. I trust we have."

Without further ado, Morpheus gave Thanatus a solemn nod and led Hugh out of the hall, making a point of not peering into any of the alcoves as they passed. Not giving it much thought, he returned them to Hugh's domain, rather than his own.

The oasis around the spring glowed with health and vitality in the moonlight, reassurance that hope continued to circulate and feed back on itself within the Sublunary. As soon as they materialized, Hugh slumped, the tension sliding away from his shoulders.

Without being entirely certain which of them had moved first, Morpheus found himself in his lover's arms — subject to a strange, unexpected shakiness.

"Holy shit, is it over?" Hugh asked, sounding none too steady himself.

Was it? Morpheus tightened his arms, burying his face in Hugh's hair. At some point during the evening, it had come free of its neat style, once more its usual wavy mess.

"Whether it is or not," he said, "perhaps it is finally time to look to the future, rather than the past."

For long moments, they clung to each other, each lost in their own thoughts.

Eventually, Hugh murmured, "Yeah." The word was a sigh, and afterward, he pulled back enough to meet Morpheus' eyes. He drew in a slow breath, and continued, "About that. I've been thinking. There's one more thing I feel like we really need to do. But first, I'll need to borrow something from your throne room, if that's okay."

EPILOGUE

HUGH HADN'T BEEN at all sure that Morpheus would go along with his crazy idea... especially since it required giving up one of the magic mirrors that hung on the walls at the center of his palace. In fact, he hadn't even known if what he had planned could work.

"You're certain you wish to do this?" Morpheus asked, still sounding understandably skeptical of the whole thing.

But Hugh had been certain from the moment the idea had come to him. "As long as you're one-hundred percent confident that you've altered this thing so it only acts as a window, not a doorway."

His lover's expression turned wry. "Believe me. I would not even be contemplating such a thing, were there any possibility that the spellwork could fail."

They were standing at the lip of the Pit of Tartarus, Hugh clutching the cloth-wrapped mirror beneath his arm. Far below, the angry wails of gigantic, trapped beasts echoed distantly.

"Then I'm sure," he said. "Come on, let's go."

Taking Morpheus' extended hand with his free one, he allowed the God of Dreams to transport them to a place he had visited twice before... a place where no one in their right mind should want to return voluntarily.

They materialized in the directionless darkness of Death's deepest realm. The void was broken only by a gifted flame that flickered and crackled, sending out a small circle of light. Around them, roars and shrieks of despair rose and fell, vibrating through Hugh's ribcage.

Then, the monstrous cries quieted. Looming shapes closed around them, sending gooseflesh up the length of Hugh's spine. This was the first time he'd been in the presence of the monsters in the pit while in his right mind... *and* his right body. He wasn't certain whether it was better or worse than being a disembodied spirit.

It was certainly more *immediate*.

"Greetings, O Titans," Morpheus called, his voice piercing the stifling gloom.

There was a pause as the great creatures leaned over them, peering down in the circle of light.

"Little godlings," rumbled a massive Cyclopes, its single eye blinking in the firelight. "Why do you disturb our torment?"

Morpheus did not hesitate. "My lover, the new God of Hope, wishes to bestow a gift, in thanks for your wisdom and assistance."

"A gift?" chittered one of the Hundred-Handers.

Hugh cleared his throat and stepped forward, lifting the mirror and sweeping the cloth from its surface. "Yes. I, um—I thought having a window into the outside world might make the time pass more quickly for you. This mirror allows you to see into the mortal realm."

The Cyclopes tilted its head, examining him like a bug under a microscope.

"Time is time," it said, in a voice like boulders scraping together.

"I suppose that's true," Hugh replied gamely. "But I find it passes more pleasantly with something to do."

"Ah," said the Cyclopes. "You seek to give us the gift of hope, as is your function."

Hugh swallowed. "I… suppose so?"

"You are young yet," it said. "You will learn in time that hope can be cruel, as well as kind."

Hugh thought back over eight hundred years of struggle and yearning; hope and disappointment. "Yes. I guess it can." He hesitated. "It wasn't my intention to offend you. I understand if—"

"We will accept your gift." The Cyclopes cut him off.

"Oh." Hugh took a step forward. "Well, I'm glad. Here, apparently you can just sort of…"

Awkwardly, he lifted the mirror into position within the circle of firelight, the cloth cover draped over his arm like a waiter at a five-star restaurant. The reflective oval caught on nothing, hanging in thin air as he took his hands away.

"There," he said.

Through the glass, a serene view of a small town beneath the light of a crescent moon showed, as clear as though it was being viewed through a freshly cleaned window.

"You are a worthy successor to your role," said the Hundred-Hander, scraping several of its insect-like appendages together. The massive creatures huddled in a half-circle, all looking at the first new vista they'd seen in untold millennia.

"I try," Hugh said.

"You do more than that," Morpheus murmured, brushing his hand and tangling their fingers together.

———◆———

Sometime later, after Morpheus had swept them away from Tartarus' freezing pit with its gifts of flame and hope, they stood at the edge of his domain, a place Hugh had only seen fleetingly before now.

The Night Land's poppy fields stretched out in rolling waves of red and purple, disappearing into the distance. The first rays of sunrise were just beginning to outline the petals in halos of yellow and orange when Morpheus spoke, breaking the easy quiet.

"Do you regret any of it?" he asked, his hand still entwined with Hugh's.

A small smile played around Hugh's lips, as he thought back over a life that had already been unimaginably eventful, even before a dead god had gifted him her long-forgotten powers.

"Not a single bloody minute," Hugh said, giving the hand clasped in his a squeeze.

They looked out across a landscape erupting in gold and crimson and green, once more subsiding into contemplative silence—two figures, standing shoulder to shoulder as the new dawn broke.

Hopes and dreams, together.

finis

To discover more books by this author, visit
www.rasteffan.com